"Her book delivers laugh-out-loud moments and leaves you rooting for the former lovebirds from the onset. It's a great, quick read to get you into the holiday spirit."

—*USA Today*

"Sexy, funny, romantic and heartfelt - this book has it all - a must read."

—Author Sandy Barker

"A fast-paced, entertaining will-they-won't-they that kept me on tenterhooks to the end."

—Author Phoebe MacLeod

"A romcom full of wit, charm, sexual chemistry and brains."

—Author Laura Carter

"You will laugh, root for all the characters and fall in love with this book (possibly even Mr. Right too!)."

—Author Aimee Brown

"I highly recommend it to all you romance lovers out there."

—Author Lucy Knott

TITLES BY CAMILLA ISLEY

• • • •

PARANORMAL ROMANCE

Don't Kiss and Spell
A Match Made in Coven

STANDALONES

It Started with a Book
It's Complicated
Fool Me Twice at Christmas
Home for Christmas
A Christmas Caroline
A Sudden Crush
I Wish for You

TRUE LOVE SERIES

Not in a Billion Years
Baby, One More Time
The Love Algorithm

FUNNY FEELINGS SERIES

This Is Not a Holiday Romance

FIRST COMES LOVE SERIES

Love Connection
Opposites Attract
I Have Never
A Christmas Date
The Love Theorem
Love Quest
The Love Proposal
Love To Hate You

JUST FRIENDS SERIES

Let's Be Just Friends
Friend Zone
My Best Friend's Boyfriend
I Don't Want To Be Friends

DON'T KISS AND SPELL

a novel

CAMILLA ISLEY

FIRST EDITION

Digital Edition October 2024 ISBN: 978 8 8872 6997 0

Print ISBN: 978 8 8872 6998 7

Audio ISBN: 978 8 8872 6999 4

To all the women who've been called witches—may your power stir up trouble and leave them burning...

Chapter One

A Wizard, a Seer, and a Raccoon Walk into a Room

RILEY

Chief Inquisitor Riley King killed the engine of his black sedan and sighed as he picked up the bouquet of vervain flowers, briar shrubs, and a handful of sorry-I'm-late-for-Christmas-Eve-dinner-Mom, from the passenger seat.

His father had died years ago, leaving his mom a relatively young widow. And Riley felt immensely guilty whenever he let his mother down. Even if only by being forty-five minutes late for dinner—hence the flowers.

He got out of the car, taking in Glenda's apparently quiet residential neighborhood. It was a dark night, threatening snow and the end of the world. A breeze was crying down the street, whisking along battered newspapers and pieces of loosened Christmas decorations while the streetlamps overhead flickered most ominously. Riley hoped it wasn't a magic crackle storm in the making. He already had enough of a bad day as it was.

He locked his car and crossed the street toward Chiron Manor. His mother's house was considered radical, even in the witching community, both for its lack of conventionality and for its in-your-face disregard of intermixing guidelines. Upon looking at it, there was no mistaking it for a human house with its black paint and its many floors and winding turrets—one with an eight-pointed star painted just above a window. No human architect could have made such a building stand without the help of magic.

The only time of the year when the house blended seamlessly into the neighborhood was during the month of October when his mom was free to leave all her magical trinkets out in the open and pass them off as Halloween decorations.

Two months later, apparently, she had neglected to recover quite a few of those "ornaments" from the front yard. As he walked up the driveway, Riley noted at least five different violations of the Conformism Act of 1792. Good thing he didn't work for the Intermixing Department and that tonight, he was finally off duty.

Riley rang the bell, pondering the right

amount of groveling and charming he'd have to unleash on his mother.

But he needn't have worried. Like every other woman on the planet, not even Glenda King—the most renowned and trusted seer on the East Coast—could stay mad at him for long.

In fact, when she came to answer the door with her lips pressed into a thin, stern line, her expression melted in a second flat at Riley's first dashing smile.

"Mom." He pulled her into a bear hug and then gave her the bouquet. "Sorry I'm late."

Glenda gracefully accepted the flowers, taking a sniff at the blossomy scent mixed with filial guilt.

She arched an eyebrow. "Work again?"

"Yes, you wouldn't believe the amount of crazy I had to deal with today." Riley walked into the house and shut the front door. "It's like every witch and wizard in town decided to settle their personal feuds around the holidays." He hung his coat on the rack behind the door. "This year, Christmas is turning out worse than Halloween. Revenge hexes, illegal potions, bootleg charms, sanctionable curses... You name it, I had to deal with it all in the past week."

Glenda sighed and shook her head as

they walked down the hall toward the dining room. "You work too much, my dear son, just like your father."

"Don't worry, Mom." Riley wrapped an arm around her shoulders and squeezed. "I have it all under control."

"That's not why I'm sighing." Riley's mother stopped next to the round dinner table, which was laid for three, and shrugged his arm off.

Before Riley could sit, she took his hands in hers. "But, for once, I hoped you were late because of a woman."

Without waiting for a reply, she dropped his hands and moved into the kitchen, coming back two minutes later with a steaming casserole filled with a whole turkey crisped to golden perfection.

Glenda dropped the turkey in the center of the table. "You know the last girlfriend you introduced me to was Amelie in high school?"

Riley knew all too well since his mother took great pains to remind him exactly that only every single time they saw each other. And to keep in line with the tradition, he gave her the same answer he always did. "That's because I haven't met anyone special yet, but I promise you'll be the first to know when I do."

Riley had no intention of ever getting tangled in a serious relationship, not after the way his parents' marriage had ended—death, pain, solitude. But he was wise enough not to share that intel with his mom. Instead, he kept humoring her desire for a daughter-in-law.

The script went on with Glenda's next line—they still had a few to cycle through before they could eat. Glenda would remind him he wasn't getting any younger, and that if he kept waiting any longer before becoming serious about finding a wife, all the good witches his age would be taken. To which Riley would joke he'd find a witch of a different age. And finally, Glenda would conclude he'd better find one of witchling-bearing age because she wanted grandwitchlings and she *also* wasn't getting any younger.

Once all of that was taken care of, they were finally free to move on to the dinner.

Riley changed the subject as fast as he could, regaling his mother with a story about a spell gone wrong he'd been saving all week exactly for this purpose. A witch had tried to curse her date to fall in love with her but ended up making herself irresistible to all manner of insects and pixies.

He was delivering the punch line

about how the witch they'd subsequently arrested had sprouted distress antennas while in interrogation from all the itching when Myron, Glenda's raccoon familiar, sauntered into the room and took the last empty seat at the dinner table.

"The prodigal son returns," the raccoon said. "I fell asleep waiting for you."

His story ruined, Riley clenched his jaws. "Sorry, Myron, but some of us actually have to work for a living. Mom understands how important my job is."

Myron snickered. "Why the flowers then?"

"Enough," Glenda cut them off. She sliced a piece of turkey and dropped it on Myron's plate. "Can't the two of you go two minutes without bickering, not even on Christmas Eve?"

"Apparently not," Riley replied, stuffing another bite into his mouth.

Myron, momentarily distracted by the food, didn't reply at all. He used his paws to tear the meat apart and chewed on a few scraps before he spoke again. "So, Inquisitor King, what's new at the Department of Magical Justice?"

The title of inquisitor was usually used, if not with downright fear, at least with a healthy amount of respect. But not when it came out of Myron's muzzle. He somehow made the appellation sound derogatory.

"I already told my mom all the good stories. Sorry you were asleep and missed out."

Myron snickered, his black beady eyes twinkling. "Then perhaps we should talk about your love life."

And Riley had walked right into that trap. If he'd already excluded his job as a topic of conversation, his personal life was fair game.

Riley kept quiet, and Myron winked at him.

The raccoon raised his glass, asking Glenda for some Dragonfire ale, and, after taking a sip, he went on torturing Riley, whom he saw as his only competition for Glenda's affection. "Seriously, Riley? Still single at your age?" Then he turned to the woman of the house again. "You know what, Glenda? I think it's past time you gave him a reading. At least this way we'll know for sure how long we have to wait for grandwitchlings."

Between gritted teeth, Riley said, "And you know perfectly well I don't let my mother read into my future."

Myron, appearing mock-shocked,

brought his clawed black paw to his chest. "Oh, but I thought that since you were almost an hour late for Christmas dinner, maybe you'd make an exception tonight." Myron bared his fangs in a vicious smirk.

Glenda rarely took sides in their verbal sparring, but she'd also been nagging Riley for ages, desperate to delve into his future with a tarot spread.

"Riley," she said. "Why don't you let me? Just this time? It'd be the best Christmas present."

"Mom, you know I don't like the idea of knowing my future. Whatever you told me would make me go about things in a different, forced way and probably screw everything good I had coming to me."

Riley could see his mom was ready to concede to his point when Myron delivered the kiss of death. "Then let her read the cards and not tell you anything... just for her peace of mind."

Glenda's eyes shone with so much hope that Riley didn't have the heart to say no. And if his mother really told him nothing, what difference would it make what she did or didn't see in his future?

"Okay," he said. "I'll do it!"

Glenda cleared the table at the speed of light, and not even Myron protested when she took his plate away before he could finish his dinner.

Plates and cutlery were replaced by candles and crystals, and Glenda brought to the table the silver chest where she kept her most special tarots, displaying the same pride in carrying them she had shown when she'd brought over the perfectly roasted turkey not an hour earlier.

Riley's mother took the tarots out, set the chest aside, and began to shuffle. When she was satisfied, she dropped the deck of cards on the table, saying, "Cut for me please, darling?"

Without giving it too much thought, Riley split the deck into two neat halves and laid the top one next to the other.

Next, his mom made him pick three sets of three random cards from the deck. Clairvoyancy had never been one of his favorite subjects in magical school, and he'd dropped it the second the mandatory credits were over. But even he remembered three was the number of harmony. One for unity, plus two for disorder. And that nine, or three times three, was considered the number of *perfect* harmony.

But beyond that basic understanding of the process, he had no way of telling what the spread before him meant.

His mother kept a perfect poker face. Riley wasn't sure if she was just keeping true to her word or if it was a tactic to bait him into asking what she was seeing. Myron, instead, kept nodding and making "ah" and "oh" noises each time a new tarot was revealed. Riley ignored him. Without Glenda's interpretation, the raccoon was just as clueless about the meaning of the spread as Riley was.

Just as Glenda turned Riley's ninth card, his phone went off in his pocket. Feeling already more than guilty for his tardiness, Riley let it ring. Someone else could take care of whatever loose jinx the call was about.

But when the phone started ringing again mere seconds after it had stopped, Riley shifted in his chair, uncomfortable. The office never called twice unless it was something serious.

"Go ahead," Glenda said. "They wouldn't disturb you tonight if it wasn't important."

"Inquisitor King," Riley said into the phone, then his jaw tensed at what the voice on the other side said.

His only reply was a one-word question. "Where?"

"I'll be right there." He concluded the

phone call and looked up at his mother. "Mom, I—"

"You have to go," she anticipated him. "I know."

"Mom, I'm really sorry. I wouldn't leave... but it's a murder investigation. They need me."

Glenda stood up. "Riley, dear, I completely understand. Don't worry. Your job is so important. I'm glad for all that you do for the community." She had a weird softness to her voice and looked like she was making her best effort not to smile. "Don't worry about your decrepit old mother."

In all the times Riley had had to leave her earlier than planned on a work call, tonight's was by far the weirdest, most unusual reaction. No complaining, no guilt-tripping, not even genuine sorrow to see him go. Glenda seemed *elated* that Riley had to go investigate a murder.

But he already had enough mysteries to solve for one night, so he simply gathered Glenda's frail form into his arms and cajoled her a little, "You're not old, Mom." He dropped a kiss on her forehead for good measure. "And are you sure it's okay if I go?"

"*Si*, yes, *oui*... go!"

She practically pushed him out of the

house. Riley barely had time to pull her into another quick hug before Glenda shoved the front door in his face.

Riley was even more puzzled but had no time to dwell on his mom's strange behavior. The moment he stepped out of her house, he left behind his doting son role and assumed that of Essex County Chief Inquisitor.

A bell in the distance rang ten strokes.

Two hours until Christmas, and what a lousy holiday it was going to be this year.

MYRON

Myron watched Glenda escort her son to the door and then come back into the living room, humming Jingle Bells under her breath.

The raccoon stared at his witch, a little perplexed. Usually, whenever her hotshot son left on a work assignment, which happened often, Glenda got all droopy and moody, but tonight, she was dancing on air.

"You seem awfully chirp for a mother whose son arrived late for Christmas Eve's dinner and left early on top of that."

"Myron, Myron," she sing sang. "Have

you looked at the cards?"

Of course, he had. But Glenda also knew that he lacked the powers of divination to correctly interpret the spread without her help. He took another look at the three tidy rows. "Care to enlighten me?"

"Look at the last row, Myron." Glenda sat back down at the table and tapped the line of cards at the bottom of the spread. "Can't you see why I'm so happy?"

The raccoon studied the cards lined on the last row: Justice, The Lovers, and The Moon.

"What do they mean?"

Glenda clapped her hands, smiling. "That my Riley is going to arrest his one true love before the night is over."

Myron furrowed his brow, even more perplexed. "Should I remind you he just left on a *murder* investigation?"

"Oh, please. Have a little faith, you old, grumpy raccoon." With one last adoring look at the tarots spread on the table, Glenda collected them in her hands and put the deck back into its honorary silver chest. "I bet it'll be a great story to tell my grandwitchlings one day..."

"Will they be born in prison?" Myron snickered.

"Don't be a Scrooge, Myron," she chided him. "Love is in the air tonight. I can feel it in my old witch bones."

And even Myron knew not to contest Glenda's premonitions, not when her old witch bones were called upon.

Chapter Two

What's in a Potion?

MILA

Mila's familiar, Abel Pawington III—or Abby for close friends and family—jumped on the kitchen counter next to where she was working, bristling his whiskers skeptically. "Mila, your magical baking license is expired." He was using his lawyer tone, Mila noted. "You can't bake chocolate love muffins."

"These aren't muffins. They're cupcakes," Mila replied, licking a smear of dark batter off her thumb.

The black cat scratched behind his ear with a paw, visibly unimpressed by her answer. "Different baked goods, same issue."

"Oh, come on, a little love potion never killed anyone." Mila kissed the top of his head. "And it's for personal use only, so it's allowed."

"And I'd respect that argument if you were making just *one* muffin—cupcake, whatever the thing—but it looks like you're mixing enough dough to feed an army."

Mila just smirked and kept adding ingredients, throwing in an extra sprinkle of sugar. "I poured too much flour the first time by accident, and I didn't want to start over or waste the batter. So I just kept adding stuff."

The mis-pouring might've happened a few times, in fact. She had added too much flour to begin with, making the batter too thick, and had had to compensate by adding more eggs and a bit more love potion, but then the batter had become too liquid so she'd added more flour and so on. By the time she'd reached the perfect consistency, she'd indeed whipped enough dough to feed, if not an army, at least half the small town of Salem, Massachusetts where she lived.

But Abby didn't need to know all the details. Mila scratched the cat under his chin to mollify him. He stood rigid at first, doing his best not to purr and keep his reprimanding façade on, Mila assumed. But eventually, she wore his stubbornness down, and his animal side took over. Purring loudly, Abby bumped his head against Mila's hand and curled himself against her arm.

Satisfied, the witch let him go and went back to mixing the dark batter in a hot-pink bowl. "You worry too much,

Abby. If not eaten, the love potion is going to lose its power by midnight, and I'm not planning on going anywhere tonight, so... no harm done. I'm just going to eat one cupcake and save the rest for the family Christmas meal tomorrow when my pastries will be just regular, delicious, magic-free chocolate cupcakes with vanilla frosting."

Abel sighed. "Mila, I know the holidays can be difficult as a single, twenty-nine-year-old witch, but a love potion...? Come on, that's—"

Mila tapped his head with a wooden spoon, leaving smears of chocolate batter on his shiny black fur. "Don't say desperate!"

Abel lifted his paw as if his first instinct had been to clean himself and lick the batter off, but then he must've remembered the love potion mixed in because he froze with his paw in mid-air.

"Afraid of accidentally bumping into the Siberian Tabby lady next door and losing your mind over a bushy tail?" Mila teased him.

"That lady cat is hateful," Abel replied indignantly.

"Sour grapes much?"

"Stop teasing me. I don't like her," he protested. "You got batter on my fur. Can you get it off?"

Mila rolled her eyes in an exaggerated gesture as if to say *"you over-fussy little creature,"* but she still wet a kitchen towel and lovingly brushed the minuscule smear of batter off of Abel's thick head.

Despite himself, she imagined, the familiar went back to purring.

Cat cleaned up, Mila finished mixing the batter and spooned it into paper cases, filling each one carefully with just the right amount of chocolate gooeyness and then depositing each case into a dedicated hollow in a muffin-baking tray. Once she had two metal trays stuffed to capacity, Mila smiled widely at her handiwork. She placed the two trays into the pre-heated oven and set a timer for twenty minutes. While she waited for the base to cook, Mila started working on the frosting.

Soon, the aroma of melting sugar and chocolate wafted deliciously throughout the entire kitchen, mixing with the vanilla spice of the frosting.

Mila hummed to herself as she measured out the powdered sugar and butter for the frosting, whipping them until they turned into a solid, sweet cloud. She set the frosting aside and checked on the cupcakes. They were rising nicely and almost ready.

Soon afterward, the timer on her phone buzzed loudly to signal that the cupcakes were cooked. She took the trays out of the oven and carefully transferred each cupcake onto a cooling rack. She helped the cooling process along by blowing a magical, icy wind over them.

The frosting was next. Mila transferred the creamy vanilla mix into a pastry syringe and squeezed it into buttery curls over the pastries, whispering the final magic incantations as she went—and ignoring the disapproving glances of her cat all the more intently.

Abby's whiskers kept twitching with worry, while his tail wouldn't sit still. The cat's displeasure was as clear as his fur was black. But as Mila finished decorating each cupcake with the white frosting and a sprinkle of silver glitter to give them a festive touch, even Abel had to admit the cupcakes looked perfect. "Those look amazing. I really don't understand why you gave up baking."

Mila's stomach grumbled hungrily, and she reached for a spatula to scoop up the leftover frosting from the bowl. The delicate sweetness melted in her mouth, and a smile spread across her lips. "I gave up baking because I was tired of trying to please everyone else with my creations," she replied. "But these cupcakes are just for me."

Mila lifted one to her mouth and was about to bite down on it when Abel yelled, "Stop."

Mila lowered the cupcake, letting out a frustrated sigh. "What now?"

"You're about to eat a love potion that will make you fall in love with the next man you see. What if it's the mailman?" Abel argued, referring to the sixty-year-old, married, balding, slightly overweight man who delivered their post.

Mila shrugged. "There's no post on Christmas Day."

"You know what I mean, what if the first guy you see is a total creep, or a serial killer, or someone you already know and can't stand, or worse, someone who's already taken?"

Mila smiled and patted his head. "Not how the magic works. The love potion is going to make sure the next man I meet *is* my perfect match."

"Yeah, because everyone knows love potions never backfire. Tomorrow is Christmas. Who are you even going to see who's not related to you?"

Mila stared out the window at the street, glittering with Christmas lights. "I could slip on the snowy curb on the way to my parents', and a handsome stranger could save me, gently grabbing me by the elbow and preventing me from falling. Our eyes would meet while he held me in his strong arms and the rest would be history." Mila batted her lashes dreamingly. "Or maybe I'll meet someone at the Christmas market downtown. My one true love and I will reach for the same pomegranate, and our fingers will brush, sending tingles up our arms. He'll offer me the pomegranate, I'll refuse and—"

"You've been watching too many rom-coms," Abel interrupted her. "You're starting to sound delusional."

Mila grinned. "Maybe I am. But can you blame me? It's Christmas, the time of miracles and magic."

Abel snorted, rolling his eyes, but didn't push further. Over the years, he had learned there was no dissuading her when Mila had her mind set on something. And she appreciated him all the more for it.

Finally, Mila took a small bite out of the cupcake, then another. The chocolate was rich and decadent, and the frosting sweet and creamy. As she chewed, she felt a warm tingle spread through her body, starting at her toes and working its way up to her scalp.

Abel watched her with concerned yellow eyes as she finished the cupcake. "How did it taste?"

Mila smiled, feeling giddy. "Like a dream coming true."

Abel rolled his eyes again. "So, what now?"

Mila bent down and kissed his furry head. "Now I'm going to take a bath. I wouldn't want to stink when I meet Mr. Right."

Chapter Three

Stunning and Stunned

RILEY

Riley took shelter behind one of the trees lining the dark street in the quiet Salem residential neighborhood. He observed the house that was his target from his shaded spot, gesturing for the other magical enforcement agents to line up behind him and blend in with the shadows.

The one-story house looked remarkably bland to belong to a witch. Nothing about its white siding, small porch, and well-manicured lawn betrayed it as the dwelling of a dangerous sorceress. With Christmas fairy lights neatly lining the porch and a sparkly plastic reindeer in the front yard, the illusion of normalcy was almost perfect. The only giveaway that revealed the building for what it really was happened to be the broomstick casually draped against the front porch. That was no human broom, and the witch definitely didn't use it to brush fallen leaves off her driveway.

An air of innocence or not, Riley knew better than to base his judgment on appearances. Years in the magical force had taught him how misleading first impressions could be. He signaled for Agent Callidora to take care of the broomstick, thus cutting off a potential escape route for the witch. Once she had the broom, Riley took a deep breath and signaled to the rest of his team to follow him as he moved ahead, slowly approaching the house on silent feet. They had to be careful not to alert the witch of their presence before they were ready to take her in.

As the two agents still with him neared the front door, Riley unsheathed his stunner gun. The weapon wasn't lethal, but one shot to the chest would impair the witch's magic long enough for Riley and his team to apprehend her. But he hoped it wouldn't come to that and that she'd go quietly.

One of the agents positioned himself by the front door, ready to kick it down at any moment. While the other waited in tense silence for Riley's signal to attack.

Riley made them wait. A kicked-down door would alert anyone inside the house to their presence and potentially make the arrest more difficult. Instead, he retrieved from a pocket in his spell-proof jacket a small, silver key with intricate engravings that glowed faintly blue in response to Riley's touch.

Riley pressed the skeleton key into the front door lock and sighed in relief when he heard it click as he turned the key. The witch, at least, had not warded the entrance with black magic or some other nasty trick.

Still on high alert, he pushed the door open to reveal what appeared to be an unassuming living room, illuminated only by the dying embers of a fire in the fireplace at the back of the room.

The house still smelled like chocolate and vanilla, making it all the more clear Riley and his agents were in the right place.

Before proceeding inside, Riley scanned the room to locate potential threats. At first glance, all he could make out were the hardwood floors, the couch, an armchair, and a small table. Then he did a double take, noticing the black mass on the armchair and its regular breathing. A cat—no, most probably a familiar—most female witches kept them. Better to subdue the animal, too.

He flipped his fingers, beckoning Malatesta, one of the two agents following him, to deal with the cat, and silently instructed the other to proceed along the dark corridor that split the house in two. They'd have to go room by room.

Riley was already moving when he heard a faint hiss, a brief scuffling noise, and then nothing. Meaning the cat had been successfully seized. He looked behind his shoulder and saw Malatesta walk out of the house holding a black sack that was shaking as if it had a life of its own. His deputy would bring the cat back to the magical law enforcement van parked outside and then rejoin them.

Riley approached the first door on the left and signaled for Agent Morales to take the one at the end of the hall. Once he was sure his deputy had understood the instructions, Riley tried the handle on the door closest to him. It was unlocked, so he slowly pushed it open to reveal a simple bedroom. A queen bed, twin nightstands on either side, a basket of unfolded laundry on top, and a chest of drawers in front of it—all faintly illuminated by the moonlight filtering in through the window. No murderous witches in sight.

He was about to check the room on the opposite side of the hall when he heard the stunner gun go off. Riley rushed to the end of the narrow corridor where Agent Morales had just discharged his service weapon. He was expecting to come in contact with all kinds of monstrous beings, seeing how black magic disfigured the bodies of its wielders in horrendous ways, and thus entered the bathroom thoroughly unprepared for the sight that awaited him.

A beautiful young woman with pearly white skin—the witch they were after presumably—was slung into the bathtub completely naked. Of course, she was naked. How else would one take a bath? She had a set of white headphones on, two slices of cucumber covering her eyes, and her long hair was floating about in the water, surrounding her like a sea of ruby-brown silk.

She was also slowly slumping underwater.

Before the water reached her nose, Riley shoved Morales aside, and, doing his best to look as little as possible at the naked body of the witch, he scooped her up from the tub.

Water dripped all over him as he turned to his deputy in an angry jerk. "Why did you stun her? Did she try to resist arrest?"

Morales looked at the floor in shame.

"Sorry, boss, I think she was actually sleeping, but I got scared and acted on instinct."

"You got scared *by what*?"

Morales pitifully gestured to the two slices of cucumber now floating aimlessly in the tub. He must've thought the witch was trying to enthrall him or something—a rookie mistake.

Before Riley could tell his deputy off, the witch came to in his arms. She coughed out a little water and began to squirm against his chest, making it all the harder to ignore how naked she presently was. Her eyes opened, revealing stunning green irises. Her expression quickly switched from confused to scared, and she started struggling to get free of his grip.

"Easy now," he said in what he hoped was a calming voice. "You've been stunned."

"Stunned?" The witch repeated in a voice still raspy from the coughing, but that Riley couldn't help but notice sounded melodic.

Then she looked down at herself, probably realizing for the first time she was being held by a stranger while completely naked, and yelped. Riley struggled not to trail the witch's gaze down her body, and soon, he was too busy containing her to worry about her bouncing breasts as she fought to get free of him.

"Easy," he repeated, using a more authoritarian tone. "I'm going to put you down now, so you can cover yourself, but try anything funny and I'm going to have to stun you again."

Fire came alive in those green irises. "Who the hell are you, and why did you stun me in the first place?" she spat.

"Chief Inquisitor Riley King, and you, Miss Bennet, are under arrest."

Chapter Four

Chief Troll of Trollery Trolls

MILA

At the Inquisitor's words, Mila's brain struggled between the urgency of performing two tasks at the same time: covering herself versus gathering enough magic to turn the annoyingly handsome, tall man holding her captive in his muscular arms into a toad.

Against any logic, Mila tried to gather what little magic she still had access to. A feeble attempt since her fingertips barely sparkled before sputtering down like an engine with no fuel. No magic flowed through her. The familiar sensation of power gathering within her core was absent. She was truly and completely drained.

The attempt, however, didn't escape her captor's hard black stare. "I said not to try anything."

He unceremoniously dropped her to her feet. Unfortunately, the shift in position added insult to injury seeing how now she found herself with her naked back pressed against his very hard front while he, keeping her in place with a firm hand on her shoulder, reached past her to pull her bathrobe off its hook on the wall.

The indignity of the pose at least was short-lived as the magical law enforcer draped the fluffy pink robe over her shoulders, purposely shoved her arms into the sleeves, and then took a petulant step back.

Mila had barely had time to register the fact that she was dressed, that he was already restraining her with iron shackles—their closing click alerted her to their presence around her wrists.

Chief Asshole Riley King now looked down at her from his six feet whatever million inches with an air of contempt and, pointing at the gaping robe, said, "You can close that up now."

Mila seethed with suppressed fury, but still thought it more practical to cover herself up—save what little decorum she had left. Only when she tried to knot her belt, the handcuffs made the job impossible.

Even more frustrated, she lifted her arms and gave her wrists a shake for more emphasis. "It's a little hard with these things around my wrists."

Mr. Chief Enforcer stepped forward

and grabbed the lapels of Mila's robe, pulling them together whilst never dropping his gaze from hers. His eyes were as black as a moonless night. He had straight black hair that fell over his forehead in a sexy curtain, a pronounced jaw, and sharp cheekbones that could probably cut through moonstone. While his lips were just the opposite, full and sensual, they looked just the right amount of soft, pillowy perfection.

Mila tried to maintain a look of sheer contempt as he gathered the robe belt in his hands and neatly tied it over her waist, but the weirdest warmth started spreading all over her body, making her more surprised than angry. If the tingling in her body wasn't magic, it sure was something similar.

Mr. Big Cop seemed equally stunned because he secured her belt in place with a tug and took a sharp step back, drawing in a gasp of air.

Mila stood lost in his dark gaze for a few more heartbeats before the enormity of the situation came crashing down on her and more practical problems took precedence over ogling the model of dark virility in front of her. "Why am I being arrested?"

The question seemed enough to shock

him into acting like a mean goblin again. Instead of answering her, he started reciting her rights. "Miss Bennet, you have the right to remain silent. Anything you say can and will be used against you in a court of magical law. You have the right to an attorney. If you cannot afford one, representation will be provided for you. Do you understand the rights I have just read to you? With these rights in mind, do you still wish to speak to me?"

"If it's not to turn you into a green slimy toad, no, I do not wish to speak to you."

"Very well, we can go then."

"Go where?"

"DMJ headquarters."

He gently grabbed her by the elbow and made to pull her out of the bathroom, but Mila shrugged him off. "Do you seriously mean to drag me to the Department of Magical Justice while I'm only wearing a robe?"

"Yes," he replied curtly.

"It's winter. I'm going to freeze if you make me walk outside in a robe with wet hair."

Riley snapped his fingers, and a blanket of warm air wrapped itself around Mila. She resented the sensation, mostly because of how pleasurable it felt.

With another snap of his fingers, her hair had dried off, cascading down to her waist in soft russet-brown waves.

"All right now?"

Mila pouted. "I'd still prefer to put on some actual clothes."

"Sorry, Miss Bennet, but you've already proved unreliable and I can't risk for me or any of my officers to be turned into toads. So, if it'll please you." He gestured to the open bathroom door.

Resigned, Mila slid her feet into the feathery flamingo slippers she wore around the house and allowed the Chief Troll of Trollery Trolls to lead her out. Mercifully, the night was dark and none of her neighbors were out to witness her humiliation. Not that Mr. Big Cop here wouldn't have put a protective glamour on her and his agents to avoid detection by humans. Even so, Mila preferred not to be seen by anyone, even if they'd been preemptively obliviated.

As they stepped out onto the porch, Mila couldn't help but notice how Riley towered over her, his broad shoulders taking up most of the space. Or how nicely his long-sleeved black shirt clung to his muscular chest and shoulders under the stunner-proof jacket.

Why did this man have to be so good-looking and imposing? And wasn't he cold, parading around in the dead of winter in just a tactical shirt and a sleeveless spell-proof jacket that only covered his chest? Maybe he'd put a warming spell on himself as well.

Mila felt a twinge of annoyance at how his towering, fit, gun-striped figure made her feel small and vulnerable. But she pushed the unwanted emotions aside and instead concentrated on finding a way to get herself out of this pickle.

But first, she was distracted by the missing broomstick on her porch.

She looked around, a frown creasing her forehead. "Where's my broomstick?"

"In impound," Riley replied shortly.

"What? You can't do that!"

"I can, and I just did."

"On what grounds?"

"Security reasons."

"How am I supposed to get around?"

"If you're found guilty, means of transportation will be the least of your problems."

Mila gritted her teeth. "This is ridiculous. I demand to know what I'm being charged with."

Riley King didn't answer her right away. Instead, he led her down the deserted street, his grip on her elbow tight and unyielding. As they walked, the muscles in his arm flexed beneath his shirt sleeve. She glanced away, feeling a flush creep up her neck. Gargoyles, she was pathetic. He was arresting her, being a troll to her, and she couldn't stop getting obsessed with a few ripped muscles. Biceps weren't so special. Plenty of guys had well-defined arms...

"Attempted murder," Riley finally said, breaking the uneasy silence between them.

Mila's heart sank before she realized the absurdity of the accusation. "That's ridiculous. I've been home the entire night. I didn't try to kill anyone."

They reached the van, and Riley opened the back door and, not too chivalrously, helped her into the back—more unceremoniously shoved her in.

She hesitated for a moment, wondering if this was a trap and considering resisting him again, but Riley's stern gaze told her he wasn't in the mood for games.

Mila reluctantly climbed into the car and sat down on one of the leather benches lining the sides. Two other magical enforcement officers, a man and a woman, were already in the van. They'd sent an entire squad to take her down armed with stunner guns they hadn't hesitated to use. Not to mention the Chief Inquisitor himself was with them. These kinds of displays of force were reserved for terrorists, wielders of dark magic, and, well, murderers.

Mr. Stuck-Up wasn't kidding. She must stand accused of some truly nefarious act. Mila stared down at the iron shackles on her wrists, and it finally dawned on her how seriously in trouble she was.

Just then, a sack on the floor hissed and moved, prompting Mila to shift away from it. "What's that?" Mila asked Riley, who was already busy locking the back doors of the van.

"Mila?" the sack asked.

"Abel?" Mila turned to the sack first and then focused an accusing stare on Riley. "What have you done to my cat?"

The only answer she got was a slammed door in her face.

Chapter Five

A Long Day and an Even Longer Night

RILEY

For the entire ride to the police station, Riley tried hard to concentrate on the road and ignore the witch locked in the back of the van.

Mila Bennet was trouble. She didn't particularly look like a bloodthirsty murderer, but he was sure she was trouble just as much as he was sure Mandrake roots weren't allowed to be harvested before the spring equinox.

And yet, as he glanced at the witch in the rearview mirror, there was something strangely alluring about her. He couldn't help but remember how her pale skin had glistened as he'd scooped her out of the tub. Or how soft and warm her body had felt against his. He had seen so much of her, too much. And those green eyes were the color of a forest in the middle of summer, inviting and mysterious. Or, equally accurately, they had the same mortal hue of sweet poison.

Right, let's remember why they were

here tonight. Riley shook his head, trying to dispel any thoughts of admiration for the witch. He couldn't afford to be distracted by her.

The Chief Inquisitor tore his eyes from the back of the van and glanced at the clock on his dashboard before refocusing on the road. Twenty to midnight, and they were close to arriving at their destination. But the night wouldn't be over for much longer. He still had two suspects in custody, a gym full of 200-odd humans to be interrogated and then disremembered, and a sure-to-be-pissed-off judge to drag out of bed on Christmas Eve. Talk about a total portal straight into holidays hell.

As they pulled into the station, Riley gave orders to his officers before getting out of the van and making his way to the back. He opened the door and helped Mila out, keeping a careful eye on her as they made their way inside.

Stunned or not, she'd already tried to use her magic on him once.

It was a busy night for Salem MPD, and Riley had to navigate through a crowded room full of officers and suspects to reach his office.

But before going in and calling the judge, he had to drop off Mila to be processed. He passed her on to one of the juridical clerks with explicit instructions to be careful and not let the witch out of their sight.

He ignored the glares Mila Bennet was sending his way and, happy to be rid of her, he went into his office.

With a sigh, he picked up the phone and called Judge Templeton.

Her Honor picked up on the fourth ring, already sounding displeased. "Chief King, the last person I wanted to hear from on Christmas Eve. How can I be of service?"

Riley explained the situation and then gave his professional opinion about the case. "Your Honor, I believe an expedited hearing might be best, and I request authorization for a spatio-temporal service squad to deal with the humans still at the school and make sure everyone gets to bed before dawn none the wiser to anything out of the ordinary having happened the night before."

"You mean besides the attempted murder of an elementary school drama teacher," the judge clarified.

"I meant nothing magical—"

"I know what you meant, Chief King. I'll get dressed and teleport to the tribunal in half an hour. Have the suspects ready for interrogation."

He sensed she was ready to hang up on him, so he prompted. "Do I have authorization for the spatio-temporal service squad?"

"Yes, of course. And, Chief?"

"Yes?"

"Please do things by the book, otherwise the Intermixing Department is going to be on our backs forever, and I'd rather not deal with them on Christmas Day. Have I made myself clear?"

"Crystal, Your Honor."

Riley hung up the phone and sighed once again. He hated dealing with unaware humans, especially during the holidays. But it was his duty as Chief Inquisitor to ensure that justice was served and humanity protected from truths too big for them to handle. He leaned back in his chair and rubbed his temples, trying to ease the headache he could feel coming on.

Coffee. He needed a strong black one. This was going to be a long night. But first, he'd better get the spatio-temporal team on the case.

He got up from his chair and made his way to the squad room, where he briefed his officers on the situation and sent them to the school to get the job started.

Riley checked his watch next. Judge Templeton would be here soon, but he still had time for a cup of coffee. A nasty voice in his head mocked him that he was procrastinating to avoid a certain witch. He shoved the thought aside. Riley was coming from a long day and was about to have an even longer night. Coffee was a necessity, not a diversion.

As he made his way to the break room, he couldn't shake off the feeling that something was off with him.

You're just tired, he told himself.

The coffee from the machine was warm and bitter, exactly what he needed.

He took a few sips and let the caffeine work its magic—even if not *literal* magic. As he leaned against the counter, his eyes drifted to the clock on the wall. No more time to waste.

With a sigh, Riley drained the last of the coffee and crunched the paper cup in his hand before throwing it into the metal bin in the corner. Time to go back to Mila Bennet and drag her and her sister in front of the judge.

Chapter Six

Hell on Earth

MILA

After another impossibly humiliating fifteen minutes where Mila had had her fingerprints and mugshot taken, the juridical clerk dropped her off on a row of plastic chairs lining the police station reception area.

Mila sat forlorn for all of a second, and then her jaw dropped as she spotted her sister slumped on the row of chairs opposite hers.

Juniper's head was hanging low on her chest, and Mila couldn't tell if her sister was sleeping or stunned or just resting her eyes. Juniper looked as miserable as Mila felt, and she was also handcuffed in iron shackles, but at least she was wearing clothes.

"*Juniper,*" Mila called, using their mental bond—to share a telepathic link was a fairly frequent occurrence between magical siblings.

Her sister's head snapped up, and their eyes met. Juniper underwent a quick-fire change as her expression switched from surprised to relieved to murderous.

"What the hell are we doing in a police station?" Mila asked. *"Did you kill someone?"*

Juniper glared at her, ignoring the question and going on the offensive instead. *"What did you put into those cupcakes?"*

"Cupcakes? What cupcakes?"

"The one I found cooling on your kitchen counter."

Mila raised her eyebrows. *"You were at my house?"*

"Yes"

"When?"

"Earlier tonight."

"Why?"

"I had—"

Mila broke out of the bond the moment the chief inquisitor stepped into the corridor in all his tall arrogance, but she was a fraction of a second too late because the darn cocky officer stopped in his stride and studied her intensely—her and then Juniper.

"Officer Malatesta," Riley called in a voice of sheer authority that had Mila's toes curl a little in her flamingo slippers. "Put mental holders on these two. I suspect they share a telepathic bond."

Mila quietly seethed in her corner, hissing a mental *I hate you, you pompous ogre* at Riley. His mouth curled at the corners. *Careful, Miss Bennet, I can hear you.*

Mila's mouth gaped open as the words landed in her mind as clear as if he'd spoken them. It was impossible. Telepathic bonds took years to form. It was unheard of for two magicians to share one within an hour of meeting each other.

King must've been thinking along the same lines because the smirk died on his lips, and his jaw set in a tense lock.

How did you—Mila began to ask in her head, but the question got cut off by an officer placing a thin iron halo on her head, effectively cutting off all mind-to-mind communications.

Juniper suffered the same destiny next. Still, the haloes didn't prevent the two sisters from sharing loaded stares that conveyed unspoken messages of reciprocal sisterly rage and blame-shifting.

"Come, you two," Riley said, inviting—*ordering*—them to stand up. "The judge is ready to see you."

Mila and her sister were escorted to a separate wing of the Department of

Magical Justice that hosted the courthouse. Riley ushered them into a small courtroom whose décor was stripped to the bare minimum: the judge's bench and two desks in front of the podium, one for the prosecution and one for the defense, Mila assumed, since this was her first time being arrested.

No space for a jury, Mila noted. So, this must be a preliminary hearing where law enforcement requested permission to hold dangerous suspects in custody before formally charging them officially. Again, a supposition born of the occasional magical police procedural Mila enjoyed reading.

As she and her sister took their seats at the defense desk, Mila couldn't help but feel a sense of dread and uncertainty consume her.

"All rise, for Her Honor Judge Templeton," a voice boomed seemingly out of nowhere.

Mila's unease worsened as the judge entered the room and the woman's piercing gaze settled on Mila and her sister. Her Honor was an older woman with white hair and wrinkles etched deeply into her face, but her eyes were sharp and commanding. Mila felt like she was being scrutinized under a microscope, every thought and action being dissected and analyzed.

"Ms. Bennet and Ms. Bennet," the judge said, her voice firm and unyielding. "Against the state of Massachusetts." The judge nodded toward a very smug-looking Riley, whom Mila could now peacefully insult in her head under the protection of the iron halo. "Chief Inquisitor King has already informed me of the events of tonight—"

Mila couldn't help but scoff.

"Is something the matter, Miss Bennet?"

"I'm sorry, Your Honor, but I still don't have the faintest idea what I'm doing here."

The judge, for all her severity, looked like she was struggling hard not to roll her eyes. "Is that the case?"

Mila nodded, still quite intimidated.

Judge Templeton sighed. "Chief King, would you mind recapping the events of the night for the sake of all parties present?"

That's when the courtroom doors banged open, and Abel strutted inside, silent on his black paws.

This time, the judge *did* roll her eyes. "What now?"

"Your Honor," Abel started. "I

apologize for the tardiness but I've been otherwise *detained*." The cat shot daggers at the chief of magical police.

"And who might you be?"

"Abel Pawington the third."

The judge stared down at him, unimpressed.

"I'm the Bennet's family lawyer."

"He's her familiar," Riley injected, pointing a finger at Mila.

"I'm a certified member of the board of animagical solicitors and therefore entitled to represent my clients in a court of law."

Judge Templeton waved them off. "The cat can stay. Chief King, please proceed with your summary of the events."

Mila soured as Mr. Arrogant stood up and started his account. "Your Honor, earlier this evening, one of our officers received a distress warning for an unusual amount of magically induced infatuations taking place at Swift River Elementary School. The Salem MPD agents who arrived on the premises initially assumed the case to be a standard violation of the magical conduct code and could trace the source of the infatuation to a set of cupcakes containing an illegal love potion."

Mila felt the gaze of her sister burn a

hole into her left cheek, but she kept her gaze pointedly trained ahead. If Juniper had stolen her cupcakes and brought them to school without asking for permission, it wasn't Mila's fault. Her older sister was a thief and had no right to stare down at her from a high horse.

"The officers were already working at damage containment, when a teacher, after ingesting one of the aforementioned cupcakes, suddenly fell ill and was brought away in an ambulance. The initial toxicology report showed the cupcake had been poisoned. Upon learning this, my agents arrested Miss Bennet Senior as she was the one who'd brought the drugged cupcakes to school and later arrested her sister, Miss Mila Bennet, as the baker and brewer of the illegal potion."

"So, what are your requests?" the judge asked.

"We request to keep both Bennet sisters in custody until formal charges can be filed."

This time, Mila did her best to contain the scoff ready to bubble out of her mouth. She had a feeling the judge wouldn't let it slide a second time.

In fact, the judge turned to her now, "Miss Bennet, did you bake the cupcakes?"

"Yes."

"And did you also imbue them with an illegal love potion?"

"Yes, but—"

The judge raised her hand. "A simple yes or no question." She turned to Mila's sister next. "And you brought the cupcakes to school?"

"Yes, but I had no idea—"

"Also a yes or no question. So, you've admitted to illegal baking and contraband of Class B magical substances," the judge stated, looking back at Mila. "How do you plead to the accusation of attempted murder?"

"Innocent," both Mila and her sister said at the same time.

"I see." The judge sagged back in her chair. "I don't know why, but I tend to believe you."

"Your Honor—" Chief King started to protest, but it was his turn to be silenced.

"Let's hear what the witches have to say in their defense first, Chief King."

"Miss Bennet, why did you bake a batch of illegal love cupcakes?"

"Your Honor, if I may," Abel interjected before Mila could reply.

"You may." The judge sighed.

"My client's baking license is merely

expired. She wasn't baking illegally and is liable to an administrative fee at most. No criminal charges should be brought forward on the grounds of illegal baking."

"Thank you, Mr. Pawington, but I'm the judge. I'll decide what punishment I see fit. Now, Miss Bennet, what's got you brewing a love potion on Christmas Eve of all nights?"

Mila squirmed under the inquisitive stare of the judge, suddenly hyper-aware of Tall, Dark, and Trollery presence on the other side of the room.

"Come on, dear," the judge encouraged, "you're standing before me in a fluffy pink robe and feathery slippers... it can't get much worse."

Oh, but it could get worse because what Mila had to say was the low point of all the humiliations she'd already suffered that night. "I was feeling lonely," she said in a mortified tone, sure, even without looking, that Riley's startling dark eyes were fixed on her. "The holidays are especially difficult for, you know..."

"I *don't* know."

"For single witches," Mila admitted, her mortification complete. "And so, I..."

"You thought you'd give yourself a little leg-up with a bit of a love potion. But why bake two trays of them?"

"I poured too much flour in the mix and had to keep adding ingredients to compensate. But the potion effect was going to expire at midnight, so I thought I'd just bring the rest of the cupcakes over for Christmas at my family's tomorrow once the magic had seeped out. I never meant for anyone to get intoxicated on my love potion."

"This brings us to how the cupcakes arrived at school." The judge turned her stare on Juniper now. "This is where you come in."

Mila stared at her sister as Juniper, nervously wringing her fingers, gave her account of events.

"I was supposed to bake cookies for my daughter's Christmas recital and forgot. And I could've gone to the store and bought some, but the Stepford wives at my daughter's school are very judgmental. They would've sniffed store-bought baked goods from a mile away. And my sister is an exceptional baker. She always has something in the oven— so to speak."

"So, you went to her house and just took the incriminated cupcakes?"

Juniper nodded.

"Why didn't you ask me first?" Mila asked.

"You were nowhere to be found, and I never imagined you'd brew a batch of love cupcakes."

"I was taking a bath, and *I* never would've imagined you'd just steal my cupcakes without saying a word."

The judge ignored the sisters' bickering and turned her attention to Abel instead. "And where were you in all this?"

"Probably licking his butt somewhere," Riley snickered, low enough for the judge not to hear him.

"I believe I was chasing mice," Abel replied with an air of extreme feline composure.

Judge Templeton massaged her temples. "Chief King, after hearing all this, do you still wish to charge the Bennet sisters with attempted murder?"

"Your Honor, at the moment, we can't exclude anything."

"You're a preposterous—" Mila started.

"Miss Bennet, please don't make your situation worse. Mr. Pawington, do you have anything to add?"

"Yes, I would like to ask Chief King a few questions if it pleases the court."

"I can't say it will please me." Judge Templeton looked more resigned than ever. "But go ahead." She waved at him.

"Chief Inquisitor King, to the best of your knowledge, were all the cupcakes poisoned, or just one?"

"Only one person was taken ill after eating a cupcake, but we're still examining the remaining ones for traces of poison."

Abel strutted confidently up and down the defense desk. "And was the poison in question human poison or a magical concoction?"

"The first toxicology report indicates regular human poison," His Arrogance confirmed between gritted teeth.

"What kind of poison?"

"Ricin."

"Is the teacher who took ill still alive?"

"She is, barely."

Able let the words hang in a moment of dramatic suspense before he asked, "Well, shouldn't she be dead?"

The room fell silent as all eyes turned to Chief King. Riley cleared his throat— finally not looking so smug anymore— and continued, "Fortunately for her, Mrs. Blackwell was rushed to the hospital in time and managed to stay alive."

Abel didn't miss a beat. "Do victims of ricin poisoning often survive?"

Chief King paused for a moment before

continuing. "No. Not to my knowledge, no."

"Didn't you wonder why the victim didn't fall dead from respiratory and organ failure before she even made it to the hospital?"

Riley ground his teeth, and Mila secretly enjoyed his squirming. Or not so secretly, given the glare the Chief Inquisitor sent her way.

"No, I haven't had time to *wonder*. It's been a pretty busy night."

"Thank you for your service, Chief Inquisitor King. Your input has been invaluable." Abel gave Riley a sarcastic nod and then turned to face the judge. "Your Honor, it seems obvious to me that my clients should be praised for having saved a life instead of standing accused of wanting to take one."

"How do you mean?" the judge inquired.

"Ricin is a deadly poison, a *human* poison. It seems logic to conclude that the only reason the teacher in question is still breathing is my client. The love potion contained in the cupcake must've counterbalanced the deadly effects of the poison, posing as an antidote of sorts. After all, love is the greater magical force on this planet, capable of defeating even death. So my question is, why would my client poison someone while providing also an antidote at the same time?"

The judge sat pensively for a second. "Sound question. Chief Riley, do you have a counter argument?"

"The older sister didn't know about the love potion. She could've still brought the cupcake to school and poisoned it."

"Except I didn't," Juniper sputtered. "I had no motive. And the cupcakes were on display all night. Anyone could've poisoned one of them."

"Including you," Riley rebuked.

"Your Honor." Juniper turned to the judge. "I'd like to take a solemn oath that I didn't poison anyone."

Solemn oaths were the ultimate line of defense for innocent witches on trial. Lie while under the effects of the oath, and the oath-breaker would die.

"No need, Miss Bennet, the fact that you offered to take the oath is enough for me to believe you. Now, I imagine you have a daughter waiting to be put to bed?"

"Yes, Your Honor."

"Then I suggest you go home and remember to bake your own cookies next time. You're dismissed."

"Thank you, Your Honor."

Mila started to also thank the judge when the woman cut her short. "Not so fast, the other Miss Bennet. While I also don't suppose you were involved in the attempted murder, you're still responsible for brewing an unsanctioned potion and then leaving the crucibles of such potent magic unattended. Chief King?"

"Yes, Your Honor."

"How hard is it going to be for your team to interrogate and disremember all the humans present at the recital tonight?"

"Extremely, Your Honor, not to mention we're short-staffed for the holidays."

That snake, he was trying to make her punishment harsher on purpose. Mila should turn him into a dung beetle. Being a toad would be too light a destiny.

"You've wreaked quite the havoc, Miss Bennet," the judge continued undeterred, shuffling some papers on her bench. "I see from your file that besides an expired baking license, you also have an equally expired private investigator one, not to mention an expired spell-weaver permit, and a magical advisor habilitation—*also* expired. Is that correct?"

"Yes, Your Honor." Mila cringed at her

lack of a clear career path being so publicly displayed.

"Well, consider your PI license renewed effective immediately. Your sentencing for the baking of a love potion with an expired license and without proper care of the resulting goods will be community service." Mila was tempted to sigh in relief, but then the judge paused for effect, her gaze swinging to Chief Riley first and Mila afterward. And Mila could've sworn she'd detected a hint of mischief in the old woman's eyes. "As part of your service, you will aid Chief Riley in clearing tonight's mess and assist him in the investigation of the attempted murder of Mrs. Josephine Blackwell until the case is solved." The judge brought down her gavel, effectively sentencing Mila to hell on earth.

Chapter Seven

Mermaid Hair and Sea Turds

RILEY

Riley heard the sentence and jumped up from his chair, ready to protest. Magical rulings were binding, which meant he wouldn't be able to put in a single minute of case work without involving Mila Bennet.

He was about to formally complain when Judge Templeton struck preemptively. "All sentencings are final, Chief Riley, so I suggest you lend Miss Bennet a uniform and you two get back to Swift River Elementary and get this mess sorted." Her Honor stood up as well. "And now, if you'll excuse me, I'll go home and enjoy a good cup of tea before a good night's sleep," she said, before leaving the courtroom.

Riley gritted his teeth. He couldn't believe he was stuck with Mila, the same woman who had caused this mess. It felt like extra punishment on top of the already alarming workload he'd have to sort out before morning.

He turned to the witch, who was

staring at him with a mixture of resignation and defiance.

In the end, defiance prevailed. Mila lifted her shackled wrists, and sporting the most viciously sweet smile, she asked, "Do you mind taking these off, Inquisitor?"

"I don't have the keys," he lied. He could've opened them with the skeleton key in his pocket.

With two fingers, he beckoned the Bennet sisters to follow him out of the courtroom and dropped them into the care of one of the clerical officers.

"Uncuff these two," he barked, knowing he was acting like a total troll but unable to contain his temper. "The halos, too. This one—" He pointed at the older sister. "Is free to go, make her sign the paperwork, and send her home. This one," Riley's mouth automatically turned down at the corners as he focused on Mila Bennet. "Get her a civilian helper uniform and send her out front to the parking lot when she's ready."

"No need," Mila protested. "If you release my broomstick from impound, I can fly myself to the school when I'm ready."

"Miss Bennet," Riley flared his nostrils. "You will come to the school in an official police vehicle with me. You might not be an officer of the law, but while you serve your sentence, you report to me." He pointed at his chest with a thumb for emphasis. "Are we clear?"

She glared at him, and he was glad she was still wearing the halo blocking her thoughts, which now were sure to be a string of verbal abuse directed at him.

Mila flashed him the faux sweet smile again, "Of course, Chief Inquisitor King."

She meant to use his title sarcastically, but the mockery in her tone didn't help the shudder the words— coming out of her perfect cupid-bow mouth in that melodic voice—sent straight down to his tailbone.

"I'll be waiting outside," he informed her sternly before turning on his heel and striding out of the police station without another glance back.

Once he was out in the fresh air, far away from Mila's intoxicating presence, if just for a little while, Riley felt relieved.

But he was still so rattled by the whole affair that he started craving a vaping wand for the first time in years. But he'd given up smoking ages ago, and he wasn't about to start again now because of an insufferable witch with an intolerably bad attitude.

As he walked toward his squad car, he heard footsteps behind him. He turned around, only to find Mila Bennet jogging up to him, her long mermaid hair bouncing with every step. "Chief King," she said in a voice that was as sugary and sweet as before but still laced with sarcasm. "I didn't want you to forget about me."

He ignored the sarcasm. Riley also tried—*and failed*—to ignore how good she looked in the dark-blue department uniform. The blouse fit snugly against her curves—of which he would have an image imprinted in his brain forever—like a glove, accentuating her narrow waist and generous hips. And the pants clung to her long legs, outlining every perfect curve. Especially her shapely behind, he noted, as she walked past him.

Riley shook his head, trying to get rid of the captivating images that had formed in his mind. "I didn't forget about you, Miss Bennet," he said curtly, his tone implying there was no chance of him ever forgetting her, considering what a giant pain in his ass she was proving to be. Riley opened the passenger door to the squad car and gestured for her to enter. "Now get in."

Mila swept into the car, swishing her

hips just enough to catch Riley's attention. He forced himself to look away, focusing on the task at hand.

He got in the car from the other side and started the engine, backing out of the police station parking lot.

"So what will we have to do tonight?" Mila asked after a few minutes on the road.

Riley gripped the wheel. It was a legitimate question, but every word coming out of that woman's mouth set him on edge, so he replied, "For now, we will ride to the school, quietly. You'll get your instructions once we get there."

Mila made a derisive zipper-over-mouth gesture and didn't speak a word. Still, her reply invaded his brain clear as day. *"Got it. Me and my long, mermaid hair will keep nice and quiet."*

Riley's eyes widened, but he kept them fixated on the road ahead. Had she heard everything he'd just thought or just the mermaid hair part? He sure hoped she hadn't heard the part about her shapely behind, and shapely behind were probably the last words he should be thinking right now... la la la la la la la la la...

"Gargoyles, you really are a pervert," came her telepathic rebuff. *"I should*

definitely turn you into a toad."

And since there was no helping it, he sent an extrasensory reply of his own. *"Miss Bennet, non-consensual shapeshifting of a government official is a crime punishable with up to ten years in prison, along with the complete discharge of all magical powers."*

In the passenger seat, Mila crossed her arms over her chest. *"Then I'll turn you into something so little they will never find you."* A moment of blessed silence and then, *"I bet no one would even miss you."*

"Said the single woman brewing a love potion of desperation on Christmas Eve."

Her indignant gasp gave him a little satisfaction.

"You're a truly despicable wizard. Has anyone ever told you that?"

"Why," he scoffed sarcastically *in his head, "you deeply wound my heart, Miss Bennet."*

"You probably have no heart. Actually, a toad would be too much of a superior life form for you. I should turn you into something more basic, like a sea cucumber. They have no hearts and you already resemble a turd, anyway."

Riley almost chuckled out loud at that but caught himself just in time before replying in his head. *"They also have no ears, which would spare me having to listen to all this incessant babble."*

"You're not listening to me with your ears, so... Yes! That's what I'll do. I'll turn you into a sea turd and then place you in a pretty bowl on my windowsill and sing Taylor Swift's songs in my head at the top of my lungs just to torture you all day long."

Riley couldn't help the smile this time. That was a pretty scary means of torture.

"You bet," she replied, still not uttering a word. *"I'm a scary witch. Scarily fun. Boo-hoo."*

He was still smiling when he asked, *"Why is it you can hear every single one of my thoughts, but I can't hear yours?"*

"Well, if you stopped broadcasting every single one of those thoughts around like they were Christmas songs and you a radio station this time of the year, I wouldn't have to listen to them."

"And how do I stop broadcasting what I'm thinking?"

She turned to stare at him now. He sensed the movement but still kept his eyes trained on the dark, icy road until her voice invaded his mind again. *"Careful, Chief King, that just sounded an awful lot like you were asking for my* help."

Silence, a real one, followed, until Mila spoke again. *"It takes patience and lots of practice."*

"Where did you get all that practice?"

"I shared a room with my sister for sixteen years. If we didn't want to be in each other's heads all the time, we had to learn how to shield our minds."

Riley nodded. *"I don't have any siblings, but perhaps—"* He cut himself short and clenched his teeth together. He really needed to stop transmitting his thoughts before they turned into billboards shouting at her to read every last one of his secrets.

Riley didn't expect to be able to shut off his mind like a tap, even so, he was happy to try. He could think about other things anyway, boring stuff like the DMV office or the mound of paperwork waiting for him on his desk, or...

Wait, why couldn't she hear him while she was in the bathroom at her house?

"You'd just stunned me, jackass."

Oh, right.

"Technically, I didn't stun you," he replied. *"Morales did. I only use stunning as a last resort. But Morales is still a recruit. He made a rookie mistake. He got scared."*

"Scared of what? Me taking a nap in the bathtub?"

"It was the cucumbers." Riley mentally chuckled. *"I don't know what kind of dark magic he thought you were trying to put him under."*

"The cucumbers?" Her melodic laugh resounded in his head. It was a song on the wind. It stirred the leaves on the ground and iced his spine. At that moment, Riley King thought he understood for the first time the allure of a siren song.

"Gargoyles, you really have a thing for mermaids. Is it just me? Or did the kink start as a child as you watched Ariel in her lilac bra? No, wait, with you, I bet it was Splash *that did it. Am I right?"*

So, it was back to thinking about boring stuff like the increased number of traffic congestions on the Interstate, or how much snow they'd get this winter, or that rumor that Donatello Malatesta was trying to nab himself a Deputy Chief position just because he'd arrived to work before the sun came up this morning. What else, what else? The rock-hard mattress they'd delivered to his house and which he still hadn't gotten used to. Mattress, bed, sex... no, no, no... bad, backtrack, think about spiders, gross, unsexy spiders—

"Ew. Whatever you do, please don't think about spiders. They gross me out."

Okay, so singing it was. *"Come to me, in the night, under the full moon's light..."*

"Please, not that song either."

"What song would you like?"

"Something more beachy."

No way. The beach reminded him too much of the delicious coconut scent of her hair that had taken over the entire cabin of the car.

"Why, thank you. It's my coconut-scented shampoo." Sarcastic mental scoff. *"You caught me in the middle of a bubble bath earlier. And I think you actually wanted to say the delicious coconut scent of my loooong mermaid hair..."* She sent him a mental wink.

He was doomed. She could hear every little thing. The only solution was to keep as far away from the witch next to him as he could.

"Suits me just fine." Mila scoffed in his head again.

Thank gargoyles they were almost at the school now. Riley recited *The Laws of Magic: A Guide to the Many Uses of Wizarding Powers* in his head for the rest of the journey until they finally turned into the school's parking lot.

Riley got out of the car and inhaled a breath of cold winter air, hoping it would clear the last bits of her intoxicating scent out of his brain. Magical sentence or not, he needed to keep the witch out of his way. Well, he'd just have to stick her on disrememberance duty and be done with it.

"I heard that. Mean."

Chapter Eight

Let's Agree Not to Sniff Each Other's Butts

MILA

Mila thought it was fun to be inside the stuck-up Chief Inquisitor's head. For one, because he wasn't as stuck-up in his head. And second, she just plain enjoyed messing with him.

Also being able to hear him while he couldn't hear her unless she wanted him to, restored the power imbalance between them. It was harder to boss someone around when they could hear every little thing you thought.

The only side effect was perhaps having to listen to the sexy thoughts he was having about her. For one, because, well, the Chief Inquisitor, despite being an arrogant troll, was still remarkably gorgeous with his messy dark hair, obsidian eyes, and even darker soul.

Not to mention how tall and defined he looked—not just looked, Mila already knew exactly how fit he was after having spent a good five minutes in his arms. This made him overall very attractive, which was a problem because he was an ogre who'd shackled her, falsely accused her of attempted murder, and, worst of all, mocked her loneliness.

Not to mention, he also seemed very appalled to be having all those naughty thoughts about her, which didn't bode well.

Especially not when he was staring at her with a wicked grin. "Penny for your thoughts?"

She mentally flipped him off and could spot the exact moment the image reached his brain because he tilted his head back and laughed.

Gargoyles, that laugh! It was sexy and masculine and totally unexpected. Rough, sensual, both cruel and kind.

She could taste it on her tongue like bittersweet nectar.

Pair that with the sight of his chest shaking, the amused twinkle in his eyes, and the way his throat and Adam's apple were exposed by his tilted head, and it was just too much to handle.

Mila shook her head, trying to clear her mind and ignore the primal attraction she felt toward him.

"I don't think you have enough pennies to afford my thoughts, Chief Inquisitor."

Riley's grin only widened. He pushed himself out of the car and started walking down the school driveway toward the main entrance.

"Are you coming or not?" he called, turning his head over his shoulder.

Mila begrudgingly followed him—not at all noticing how nicely his uniform pants stretched on his derriere. Apparently, he wasn't the only one into shapely behinds.

No, nope. Not interested.

Oh, who was she kidding? As they walked, Mila couldn't stop staring— ogling, really—at the Chief Inquisitor's muscular physique, his purposeful strides, and the way he held his shoulders back, projecting a sense of confidence. It was no wonder he was so intimidating—he looked like he could take on anyone and emerge victorious. But there was something else she noticed too, something that hinted at a vulnerability beneath all that bravado. It was in the way he walked, with a slight limp in his gait, as if he were nursing an old injury. She wondered what that injury could have been.

Not your riddle to solve, she chided herself. Everything about Chief Inquisitor Riley King screamed bad idea, and she'd better remember it. Better even, she should get "bad idea" tattooed on the back of her right hand as a reminder whenever she started thinking about toned chests and nice butts.

"What's a bad idea?" Riley asked, holding the door to the school open for her.

And now she was getting sloppy with her mental shields, too. Mila glowered at him, spitting, "The bad idea was thinking you could just waltz into my life and stun me, shackle me, and then accuse me of attempted murder with no evidence."

Riley's expression turned serious as he replied, "I already told you *I* didn't stun you. As for the rest, I was only following protocol. I won't apologize for doing my job."

"So is admiring my shapely behind part of the job description?" Attack was always the best defense.

A red flush crept up his neck, visible even in the less-than-ideal lighting.

"I apologize if my thoughts have offended you. I'm not used to having to guard them."

Mila couldn't help but smirk at his discomfort. She was enjoying having the upper hand for once, even if it was just in his thoughts.

"It's fine, Chief Inquisitor," Mila said, trying to sound nonchalant. "I can handle a little ogling. But let's get one thing straight: I'm not interested in you. Not now, not ever."

Riley gave her a look that suggested he didn't believe her. "Is that so?" he said with a hint of amusement. "Because I think I also heard something about toned chests and nice butts"—he circled a finger above her forehead—"in there somewhere."

Mila sighed in an exasperated way. "Then, let's agree now that even if we both possess a butt the other appreciates, we're never going to sniff them."

Once again, Riley threw his head back and assaulted her with that rough-sensual laugh of his. "Here I solemnly swear, Miss Bennet, never *ever* to sniff your butt." Then he turned serious. "Get inside now. We have work to do."

"Yeah, I know. I'll go join the disrememberance team if you could just point me in the right direction."

"Everyone is still being held in the gym, all humans, that is. The gymnasium is down the second hall on the right, third door on—"

"This is my niece's school. I know where the gym is."

"If you're such a wonderful aunt, why weren't you at the recital?"

"Tickets are limited to five per family. I went last year. This year it was my brother's turn."

"That makes three tickets."

Mila frowned. "What do you mean, *three* tickets?"

Riley counted off his fingers. "Your sister, her husband, I assume, and your brother."

"Oh, the other two are for my parents. Try to keep my mom away from one of her grandwitchlings' events at your own peril. Do you have any more invasive, personal questions?"

"No, that'd be all, Miss Bennet."

"Fantastic. While you go do your very important investigative job, I'll go be with the low-life minions taking care of the menial stuff."

"Not a minute too soon." Riley nodded, turning on his heel. "And, Miss Bennet?" He paused, looking back at her. "Report back to me when the job's done."

"Sure, Chief Inquisitor." Mila made a mock military salute, and at the end of the flick, she turned it into a bird-flipping. "I'll be holding my breath until then."

Having put in the last word, Mila sauntered away toward the gym for a sure-to-be crappy couple of hours. But, hey, they couldn't turn out worse than the two she just had.

They could, and they did.

Chapter Nine

Not Another Fascinus Pic

MILA

Once the disrememberance team discovered that Mila was the witch who had brewed the love potion, they put her in charge of concocting an antidote. Then she'd have to administer it to all the human attendees of the recital who had eaten a cupcake and consequently fallen in love with the most improbable matches. While the rest of the disrememberance team would focus on those humans who had witnessed magic they shouldn't have.

Antidotes sucked. For one, they stunk. Then they took an excruciating amount of precision to brew properly, and patience truly wasn't Mila's forte—she'd almost failed potion class in witching school exactly for that reason. And then there was the fact that antidotes were time-sensitive, and the longer it took from the time the potion was consumed, the less effective they turned out—with the added risk of lasting damage. Hence why she had to be extra precise but also super fast.

Nevertheless, even Mila recognized she was the best person for the job. Magic had a way of recognizing itself, and antidotes brewed by the same witch who'd created the initial potion were tenfold more potent than if another witch or wizard made them. So, Mila really had no choice.

She'd tried to give her love life a little boost, and now the Cosmo was punishing her. And the worst part? She had no one to blame but herself.

She could still hear Abel's warning words, which she'd chosen to ignore, in her head. Her familiar had warned her about the risks, and she'd still taken them. Why? Because Mila had reached the point where the idea of having to go on another Spellbinder date had her so nauseated that she'd rather resort to a potion as a last-ditch effort to find love outside of a dating app. And yes, if you'd been on enough Spellbinder dates, you'd agree with her. She didn't need to receive another unsolicited Fascinus pic, thank you very much. Mila had received enough phallic charm images to last her a lifetime.

But the dating pool as a witch was limited. Mila had already tried dating a regular guy once, a non-wizard. He was sweet and charming. Had she been an ordinary gal like him, they'd probably be married by now. But she wasn't. She was a witch, and by the end of their first month together, she already had to disremember him so many times she feared that if they kept on dating, he'd get some lasting brain damage.

Taking all that into account, making a love potion had still looked like a reckless move, but the alternative had seemed, at the time, even more daunting. Now, not so much. If she'd listened to her familiar, now she could've been in bed curled up with a book, or sleeping, and *not* have a criminal record.

Oh, Abel was going to have a string of I-told-you-sos so long, she'd be listening to them until the day she turned eighty. But at least now her familiar was at home and cozy—Mila had asked Juniper to give him a lift from the police station— probably warming his paws in front of the fire. Contrary to her, who was stuck at Willow's school for the entire night brewing the smelliest antidote.

Mila could feel the exhaustion already seeping into her bones. Being stunned was no walk in the park. And neither was having to deal with Tall, Dark, and Stuck-up and all his sexy thoughts.

But Mila didn't have time to think about that right now. She needed to focus on the practical aspects of getting herself out of this mess of her own creation. And the first step was to erase any trace of her unfortunate love potioning.

After procuring all the right ingredients from the magimedic team, Mila had to spend an incredibly stressful half an hour bent over a cauldron, trying not to inhale too much of the stinky fumes as she brewed the antidote. It was tedious work, but she couldn't mess it up. Lives were at stake, after all.

But that was nothing compared to what came next: actually administering the antidote to the affected victims.

Antidotes didn't taste any better than they smelled, and a concoction whose sole purpose was to rid its drinker of amorous feelings? Well, it was bound to be truly disgusting. Add that antidote-takers couldn't be left alone for fifteen minutes after having drank the remedial potion, and Mila spent the following four hours alternatively coaxing and cajoling the victims to drink the antidote and then keeping them company while they rode out the effects.

Like with drunks, she got all kinds of

lovesick types.

Some were embarrassed, some were angry, and some were just plain sad. The worst ones, though, were the whiny variety for whom Mila had to put on her best sympathetic face and pretend she was interested in listening to their sob stories about their magically induced, unrequited love. It was exhausting, but it was her responsibility. At least *they* hadn't asked for this.

As the night dragged on, the gym emptied out as people got cured of their woes of the heart and had their memories selectively readjusted afterward.

But at least not the entire night had been a waste. While she listened to the lovesicks complain about their lives, Mila had gathered enough intelligence to pinpoint at least three suspects for the attempted murder of Mrs. Blackwell.

That knowledge put a spring in Mila's step as she crossed the gym. Even though the night had been long and tiring, she'd made some actual progress on the case, and she couldn't wait to share her findings with Mr. Big Cop. But as Riley spotted her coming and their eyes met across the basketball court, his expression told her he was less than thrilled to have to deal with her again.

He didn't seem angry, per se, but there was definitely a coolness in his gaze that hadn't been there before. So, the fun times they'd shared in the car were over, and it was back to him playing bad cop. Unbidden, an image of what Riley would look like playing bad cop in bed invaded Mila's mind. She pictured herself naked and handcuffed to a bed while he towered over her, his expression stern and unyielding as he teased and tormented her with pleasure. The thought was so unexpected she didn't even think to guard it.

Oh gargoyles, she hoped with all her soul that he hadn't received a mental image of that very inappropriate sexual fantasy. But Riley's brows knitted so close together in such a formidable scowl that Mila felt certain that he had seen *something*. And then he looked at her, eyes dark and fathomless.

She was so busted.

Chapter Ten

Fifty Shades of Witch

RILEY

Riley's night had been a hell-pit show from the start and now, after hours of conducting interviews with all those who had been present at the recital, it was clearer than ever that this was a case of ordinary human poisoning.

The Department of Magical Justice wouldn't even have been involved if it weren't for Miss Mila Bennet and her wayward love potion.

But wizardly attempted murder or not, now that the DMJ had claimed jurisdiction, the hot potato was his to deal with. They couldn't just drop the case back into the hands of the Salem Police Department.

Regular cops thought the DMJ was a federal agency that commandeered certain cases of special interest to national security—the best possible excuse not to have too many questions asked. To keep the existence of the wizarding world concealed while still maintaining the magical order was a delicate balance, and bouncing a case back and forth between human and wizarding law enforcement agencies was a huge no-no.

So here he was, stuck with this case to solve and stuck with Nancy Drew to babysit.

Speaking of the devil, he spotted Mila emerging from the room where she'd been administering antidotes all night. She looked tired, with a hint of bags under her eyes and her hair falling down to her waist in messy wisps.

But the weariness somehow worked in her favor, adding even more appeal to her natural beauty.

She caught sight of him and smiled, crossing the gym to join him. And it wasn't an especially bright smile or a suggestive one, but it still twisted something deep inside Riley's stomach. He wasn't sure if it was irritation or attraction, but he pushed the thought away before it could fully form—and before she could hear it.

She was almost by his side when the most disturbing image popped into his head. He saw Mila naked—as if he needed another reminder of how perfectly smooth and soft her body looked sans clothes—handcuffed to a bed while Riley was about to... he didn't get to see what he was about to do to naked, handcuffed Mila before the image was yanked from his brain rather violently.

Riley frowned. That was weird. Had he just freaked himself out of his own thoughts?

Then another, even more disturbing possibility sneaked into the back of his mind. Had those even been *his* thoughts?

He took one look at Mila, at the furious blush spreading on her cheeks and at how studiously she was avoiding his gaze, and he smirked.

"Miss Bennet," he said. "A word, if you don't mind."

He gently grabbed her by the elbow and dragged her out of the gym, down the hall, and then into an empty classroom where they could talk with some privacy. Not that they needed it, since this was a conversation they were about to have mind to mind.

"Gargoyles, you really have a kink for handcuffs." Riley exploded the thought down their mental bond. *"Is it just me? Or did you read too many cop romances growing up?"*

He felt a twinge of satisfaction at throwing her taunting words from earlier in the car about him having a thing for mermaids back at her.

Mila's eyes widened, and she spoke in actual words. "I'm sorry, that was inappropriate. But it's not my fault my brain went there."

Riley raised his brows. "So, it's mine?"

"You were standing there looking impossibly hot and stormy and mean, and then your expression changed to... something else." Mila trailed off, her cheeks still flushed.

Riley couldn't help the smirk that played on his lips. "Something else?"

Mila rolled her eyes. "Fine. It was a mix of desire and aggression, and it just threw me off. I thought you were playing bad cop again and then my brain just..."

"Moved the playfield to the bedroom?" Riley suggested, still smirking.

Mila groaned. "Can we just forget about this? It was a weird moment, nothing more. I'm tired."

Riley couldn't help the chuckle that escaped him. "Sure thing, Miss Bennet. We can forget about your preferences for bondage." But even as he spoke, his thoughts were far from forgetting about it.

She didn't respond. Not even a little comeback, a witty quip?

Riley cocked his head, studying her.

Her exhaustion was palpable, and he couldn't help but feel a twinge of guilt. He had been teasing her a bit too relentlessly in the car earlier, and it seemed like it had taken its toll on her.

"I'm sorry," he said honestly. "That was a low blow."

Mila waved it off, but he saw the way the corners of her lips twitched upward briefly before she returned to looking worn-out.

"I get it," she said, with a small shrug. "We're stuck together on this case, and we're going to be spending a lot of time in close proximity in the next few days. Something I'm sure we'd both rather avoid."

"Yeah, but your shift for tonight is over. Come on." He tilted his head toward the door. "I'm driving you home."

Mila rubbed her eyes and yawned. "What time is it?"

"Four a.m."

"Oh gargoyles, do you think the spatio-temporal team could spare a few time-stretching pills?"

They had, in fact, given Riley a four-hour pill that would stretch time and gain him a few extra hours of sleep. Gargoyles knew he needed to rest to get his brain straight in the morning and solve the case. But Mila looked truly bone tired. She probably needed the extra hours of sleep more than he did. "Yeah, I have a few hours' pill I can give you."

She stopped walking and looked up at him with wide, impossibly green eyes and the weirdest expression. It was part stupor, part admiration, and part something else his gut told him he'd better not explore. "You're very kind," she said. "But we can split the four-hour pill. Two extra hours of sleep will be plenty to make my brain right again."

And she could still hear every little thing he thought.

"Don't worry, you'll learn how to control what I can hear." The unspoken words were a gentle caress against his brain.

Riley swallowed hard as his eyes flicked to Mila's lips, the sudden urge to kiss her almost overwhelming his senses. He *so* needed to pull himself together and control his instincts. He'd already crossed too many lines with her today, ones that he couldn't afford to cross again. Not when they were stuck together for the foreseeable future on this case.

"After the Fifty Shades of Inappropriate image I just sent to your brain, you're fretting about wanting a kiss?" she silently asked as they navigated the

almost empty school corridors toward the exit.

Riley chuckled, trying to diffuse the tension that was building between them. "It's not just a kiss, Miss Bennet. It's the consequences of a kiss between us."

Mila looked up at him, her eyes heavy with exhaustion but still searching his face for something he couldn't quite place. "The consequences?"

"The complications," Riley clarified, running a hand through his hair. "We're partners on this case. We can't afford... distractions."

What a load of dragon droppings, he thought.

Mila smirked. "I agree on the dragon droppings. But I get what you're saying. Let's keep things simple. We can solve the case as fast as possible and then go our separate ways."

Her words made total sense but somehow still brought a sense of displeasure to his chest.

"About the case," Mila continued. "I made a few interesting discoveries tonight. I have at least three suspects."

Three? He'd barely found one, and Nancy Drew here had *three*?

Riley held the school door open for her. Mila made to scoot past him, but paused midway, looking up at him with twinkly eyes. "So, I'm Nancy Drew now?"

Riley rolled his eyes and groaned.

"I prefer Veronica Mars," he retorted with a smirk.

Mila laughed tiredly, but the sound was music to Riley's ears. "Fair enough."

He nodded in agreement, and they made their way to his car.

"Do you want to hear my theories now or tomorrow?" she asked once they were both strapped in the car.

"Tomorrow might be best." He put the car into gear and pulled onto the dark road. "Listen, I know tomorrow is Christmas and you probably have some big celebration planned—"

"Why, you don't?"

"I don't have a big family. It's just going to be my mother and me and her annoying-as-hell raccoon."

"Okay." Out of the corner of his eye, he saw Mila nod. "So?"

"I'd still rather work a few hours on the case, possibly go see if Mrs. Blackwell has awakened to ask her a few questions."

Riley felt a wave of shame that wasn't his, just as Mila said, "I didn't even ask how she was doing."

"She's being kept sedated at the moment while her body works through the effects of the poison, but the doctors are positive she'll have a full recovery. And I've put a couple of undercover agents at the hospital to guard her, should the killer decide to finish the job while she's unconscious."

"That's good, I guess."

"So, I can't work on the case unless—"

"Unless I'm with you?"

Riley nodded. Binding magical sentences were total bitches.

Mila laughed. "I know, trust me. And it's okay. I can sneak out early from the celebrations. Gargoyles know I'll have to eat so much crow about the love potion thing tomorrow. I'll probably be eager to get away."

"I'm sorry I teased you about that earlier." He sent the thought telepathically. Somehow, apologizing without actually saying the words was easier.

"It's okay," she said out loud. "It was a stupid idea, and you're right, a bit desperate, too."

Riley gritted his teeth at the word "desperate." He shouldn't have used it.

Silence descended on the car, and as they drove back to Mila's house, Riley couldn't help but steal glances at her from the corner of his eye. She had fallen asleep with her head resting against the window, and he felt a pang of protectiveness toward her.

He shook his head, trying to dispel those thoughts. This was not the time or place for any kind of attachment.

As they reached Mila's house, Riley parked the car and turned toward her, that unwanted need to protect her resurfacing with a vengeance. He didn't feel like waking her, so instead, he unbuckled her seatbelt and, circling to the other side of the car, scooped her up into his arms. Riley carried Mila up the driveway and used his skeleton key to let himself into her house, walking straight toward the bedroom he'd found on his earlier bust.

He gently deposited the sleeping witch on the bed, covering her with a fuzzy quilt. Then he went to the kitchen and filled a glass with water. He brought it back to the bedroom and helped Mila into a half-sitting position, holding her against himself and trying hard to ignore how good her weight on his chest felt.

He took the time-stretch pill and pushed it between her lips, lifting the glass of water to her mouth next.

"Drink this," he whispered, adding a

little incantation to the words to make sure she would comply even while sleeping.

She drank.

Riley made sure Mila had swallowed the pill and then tenderly lowered her onto the pillows. Before leaving, he had to battle every instinct in his body not to stamp a soft kiss on her forehead.

Instead, Chief Inquisitor Riley King quietly left the room and walked down the hallway to wash the glass of water in the kitchen, leaving it to dry next to the sink. Then he exited Mila's house, his heart pounding wildly in his chest, and drove himself home, hoping that he would be able to forget the feeling of holding Mila Bennet in his arms twice in a single night.

Chapter Eleven

Hex Me, Hex My Life

MILA

Mila woke up in her bed feeling well rested, yet somehow believing she shouldn't be that restored. Next, she tried to remember how she'd gotten into bed. The last thing she recalled was being in Riley's car, and... oh gargoyles, all the events of the previous night came crashing down on her.

Mila looked down at herself. She was still wearing her civilian uniform from the night before. She sank deeper into the pillow, bringing her quilt over herself until her entire face was covered, and she groaned.

The mattress shifted at her feet. "Hiding under the covers won't change what happened," Abel said.

She freed her face from the blanket and stared down at her feet where her familiar was methodically licking one of his paws and passing it over his ear.

"Merry Christmas," he said, and even the simple wishing sounded passive-aggressive.

Mila knew she was going to regret asking, but she did anyway. "Do you have any idea how I got into bed last night?"

Abel paused his licking and studied her with intent yellow eyes. "A certain tall, handsome inquisitor carried you inside in his arms." Mila's pulse picked up speed. She had feared as much. "Then he put you into bed, gave you a pill, and went on his way."

"An entire pill?" Mila asked remembering their conversation about the time-stretch pill. "He didn't break it in half first?"

"I'm a cat. I can see in the dark. He gave you the *entire* pill and then left."

"And you let him drug me?"

Abel shrugged. "I figured Inquisitor King is still DMJ and wouldn't slip you anything funky. Why, what did he give you?"

"A time-stretch pill," Mila said absentmindedly, finally understanding why she was feeling so rested after just a few hours' sleep and also wondering just how crappy Riley was going to feel in comparison after giving her the entire pill. "But we were supposed to share it."

Abel kept quiet. He just stared at her with a Cheshire grin.

"What?" Mila asked self-consciously.

"Someone has a crush," the cat teased.

"Don't be ridiculous." Mila threw the quilt off her legs and got up. "I don't like Riley."

The cat hopped off the bed and brushed himself against her legs. "So, it's Riley now? No longer Inquisitor King?"

He was teasing her.

"You're a wretched, wretched animal."

Mila picked up Abel and held him close to her chest, burying her face into his soft fur while he purred contentedly. "I can't have feelings for him," she muttered under her breath.

"Whatever you say, boss," Abel said, still amused.

Mila sighed. She knew that if she let herself fall for Riley, it would only end in heartbreak. He sent off anti-relationship vibes so strong that if he tried any harder, they'd tsunami the hopes of any woman even remotely interested.

She didn't even have to ask if he was single to know that he was.

Mila shook her head, trying to rid herself of these thoughts as she got dressed for the festivity. She had to focus on the day ahead and the pain it would be to explain to the entire family why she'd gotten herself and her sister arrested on Christmas Eve. Juniper was bound to be still murderous about the whole affair. Kevin, her brother, would tease her to no end. Her dad would deliver an hour-long lecture on the dangers of misusing magic. And her mom would just worry about the state of her mental health for resorting to love potions to find a partner—but on the bright side, Mama Bennet would probably at least refrain from bugging Mila about being the only unmarried one of her children. *Yay.* Small victories.

The day hadn't properly started yet, and Mila already couldn't bear it. But she had to find some way to make it through the holiday and then move on with her life.

She went into the kitchen to make herself a cup of coffee. Nothing would jolt her system better than a little caffeine.

After she showered and finished wrapping the last presents for her family, Mila still had a little time left. On impulse, she grabbed her knitting irons and a spool of black wool and began weaving a beany in the armchair next to the fireplace.

Able jumped on the armrest next to her. "What are you making?"

"A beanie."

Abel studied her handiwork. "Isn't it a little big for you? Even *your* head is not that thick."

"It's not for me," Mila replied noncommittally.

Abel dropped, resting his head on his front paws—the human equivalent of propping one's chin over one's hand. "And who might it be for?"

"Ri—Chief King."

"Christmas present?"

"No."

"Then why are you making him a hat, Miss I Don't Have A Crush?"

"Because the man can't keep a hold on his mind, and I'm tired of having to listen to all his mental nonsense."

The shrewd expression was wiped off Abel's muzzle. "You share a telepathic bond?"

Mila shrugged. "I know it's unusual, but we—"

Abel didn't wait to hear the rest. He jumped off the armchair and trotted over to the bookcase at the back of the room, using his paw to pull down a book before starting to read it.

Mila shrugged. Her familiar reading and ignoring her was a far better option than him asking uncomfortable questions. It suited her just fine. She finished knitting Riley's beanie, enhanced it with an incantation to shield the wearer's mind, and then went to get dressed for the dreaded meal at her parents' house.

She was about to head out of the house, laden with bags of presents, when Abel called after her, "Mila, hold on. I have to talk to you."

Mila shifted one of the heavy bags in her arms to have a better balance. "Sorry, but that will have to wait. I can't be late for lunch on top of everything else."

"But I have something really important to tell you."

"Okay, shoot."

"You need to sit down for this."

"Sorry, don't have the time so"—she shot him a wicked grin—"unless you want to accompany me to my parents, it'll have to wait."

"Gargoyles spare me." Abel made a disgusted face. "And have all the little witchlings pull on my tail all day long? No, thank you. I'll skip."

"Then we'll talk later, or I'm going to be late."

Mila got out of the house and let loose a string of swear words at not finding her broomstick on the porch. "Stinking pumpkins, blasted trolls, cursed cauldrons, and bleeding ghosts."

The broomstick was still in the impound. Darned dragons and festering faeries, turns out she *was* going to be late no matter what. Stinking gargoyles, hexed harpies, and pox-ridden goblins.

Mila let out a frustrated growl and headed down her street, readying herself to *walk* all the way to her parents' house in hexing December, in hexing Massachusetts, with hexing snow hexing everywhere. She almost slipped on a patch of iced-over curb and thought, hex me, hex my life.

Mila steadied herself, took a deep breath, and plowed forward, cursing all sorts of magical creatures in her head the entire way to her parents' because what other choice did she have?

Chapter Twelve

I Want to Get Away, I Want to Fly Away

RILEY

Riley woke up with a splitting headache and not nearly rested enough. Still, he didn't linger in bed. He got up, scrambled some eggs for breakfast, and popped two Advil—sometimes human remedies were just as functional as magical ones.

The moment his head stopped throbbing so much, he took his broomstick, wrapped himself in a warming spell, and went for a spin over the snowed-in town. Flying always made him feel better, more clear-headed. And today, he had many thoughts he wanted to purge from his brain—all revolving around a certain green-eyed witch with a sharp tongue and an even sharper mind.

But as he soared above the trees, Riley's thoughts inevitably drifted back to Mila. He glided over the small houses with their warm, glowing windows, and all he could see was her glowing skin. Instead of the cold misty air, her scent lingered in his nostrils, and her melodic laugh still echoed inside his skull.

A stronger gust of wind whipped through his hair, and his thoughts finally scattered like dandelion seeds carried by the breeze. For a moment, he lived only in the present, absorbed in the sensation of flight.

But as he flew on, his thoughts started to coalesce once more. First, the image of Mila's stunned expression when he'd offered her the time-stretch pill. And then, more vivid images of her soft body that he was only partly to blame for having.

That was the other thing that nagged at him, their telepathic bond. It was highly unusual. And while he couldn't do any case work without Mila by his side, as per her magical sentencing, he sure could investigate the reason their minds were linked.

He veered the broomstick toward his mother's house, hoping to find some answers in the vast collection of magical tomes Glenda had in her home library. As he landed on her front porch, Riley took a moment to compose himself, shaking off the strange mix of emotions Mila had stirred in him. The last thing he needed was for his mother to get on his case.

Still, as Glenda came to open the door, she gave him an unusually long stare. "Riley, you're early. Lunch isn't ready yet."

"Hi, Mom. Merry Christmas." He pulled her in for a hug and a kiss on the cheek. "Do you mind if I have a look in the library while we wait?"

"Not at all." She opened the door wide and let him in.

Riley gave her another kiss and went ahead to the library.

He knew exactly what section he needed to look at and went straight there, scanning the spines until he found what he was looking for. The book was old, with yellowed pages and a musty smell. He scanned the index with his finger, mentally noting the two chapters he was most interested in. The one explaining why mental bonds would form and the one giving instructions on how to block them.

Screening his thoughts from Mila seemed like the most pressing matter, so he read that chapter first and ended just as frustrated as he'd started. The book drawled on for pages, but in the end, it gave Riley the long answer to what Mila had already told him: he needed patience and lots of practice.

He was about to dwell into the section detailing the possible reasons for his mind link with Mila—the only one he had studied in school was kinship—when his mother called him to the table.

Riley sat at his usual spot opposite Myron with his mom in the middle. As they started eating, he couldn't help but notice the atmosphere had a weird charge. Glenda and Myron kept exchanging glances and eyebrow arches as if they were conducting an entirely separated conversation that excluded him. Riley was pretty sure they didn't share a telepathic bond, but he still couldn't shake the feeling they were discussing something in code, and, even more ominously, that the *something* had to do with him.

"How was work last night?" his mom finally asked.

A hell-pit show, he wanted to say, but his mother wasn't fond of swear words so he just shrugged and said, "Oh, you know, the usual."

Glenda sliced through a piece of leftover turkey from last night with her knife. "Wasn't it a murder case you were called on?"

"Attempted murder." Riley scooped up some mashed potatoes. "And it turns out the case is one-hundred percent human, but an unfortunate amount of magic was involved, so now I'm stuck with it, anyway."

Glenda and Myron exchanged another stare, and the raccoon asked, "Were there any arrests?"

Riley gulped down a sip of starlight cider before answering. "Yeah, but the witch was innocent," he said, thinking of Mila.

His mom smirked at that. "Was she by any chance beautiful, single, and of witchlings-bearing age?"

Mila definitely was all three things, but Riley would be damned before he admitted any of that to his mother. She'd jump at the chance to matchmake and plan the wedding before he had even sorted his feelings toward Mila.

He took the easy way out. "I don't think so, since the victim was her daughter's drama teacher."

Glenda's face fell. "And she was the *only* arrest you made?"

That was a weird question. Proceedings were sealed, and Glenda had no way of knowing he had, in fact, made two arrests last night. What was going on? The look on his mother's face was too intense, too keen almost.

A sinking feeling lodged into the pit of his stomach. "Mom, why are you asking that?"

"Oh, no reason." She flipped her long, white hair nonchalantly. "The Herald mentioned something about multiple suspects."

Something in her tone was definitely too casual, and since when did Glenda King read the Witchly Herald?

A sense of doom hit Riley in the chest, and he narrowed his eyes at his mother. "Mom, what did you see in my reading last night?"

"Nothing," she answered way too fast.

Years as a law enforcer and an experienced interrogator had taught Riley to smell a lie from a mile away. "Nothing? Is my future a black cloud of midnight dust, then? Because I'd rather know if I'm going to drop dead tomorrow."

"No one's dying." Glenda reached out and squeezed his arm over the table.

Riley remained skeptical. "Then what did you see?"

His mother looked him straight in the eye. "Only good things, sweet pumpkin. I promise."

The words were meant to be reassuring but they had the opposite effect, and the sense of unease that had been accompanying Riley all day intensified. Especially since it was almost time to go pick up Mila Bennet.

Chapter Thirteen

What Do Witches Put On Their Bagels?

MILA

Mila's Christmas was proving worse than her most pessimistic projections. For starters, the Witchly Herald had published a story on the elementary school poisoning, including details about the involvement of a love potion. The paper hadn't named names, but Salem was a small town and by noon, anyone in the neighborhood knew that the Bennet sisters had been arrested the previous night and why—much to their mother's chagrin.

The most humiliating part was that everyone knew it had been Mila who had brewed the love potion. Juniper was happily married to the perfect wizard. She'd have no reason to resort to magic tricks to find love.

As expected, the entire family had an opinion about the matter. Her dad was convinced that using their powers for unethical purposes would mark them forever and corrupt their souls. Her mom was more focused on Mila's emotional well-being and questioning why she couldn't find a man on her own without needing to resort to *extreme measures*—her words—like love potions.

Juniper wasn't speaking to her. The silent treatment was her sister's punishment of choice.

Mila's only bearable relative was her brother, who kept teasing her affectionately, dropping the odd wizarding joke when the atmosphere at the table became too tense.

Mila slumped lower in her seat, eyeing the food in front of her with a lack of interest. The meal felt interminable. Her mother's cooking was usually delightful, but today everything tasted bland and unappetizing. All Mila wanted to do was to get out of there and go home, but she couldn't leave. At least not until Riley came to pick her up, giving her an official excuse to flee the family gathering.

A community service sentence was as ironclad a reason to leave as they came. But that was still a few hours away.

So, Mila adopted the survival strategy of being as inconspicuous as possible, keeping quiet in her corner and joining the conversation only when addressed directly by someone, which still happened way too often.

When her uncle started a conversation about the dangers of misusing magic, Mila was ready to pull out her hair.

"Uncle Edwin." Kevin diverted his attention, coming to Mila's defense. "What do witches put on their bagels?"

The entire table turned to face Kevin, shifting the bullseye away from Mila.

Her brother waited for another heartbeat before delivering the punchline, "Scream cheese."

Everyone laughed, but still, Mila couldn't take it anymore. She excused herself from the table, pretending she had to go to the bathroom, and went outside for some fresh air instead. It had started snowing, and snowflakes were swirling down from the sky, thick and fast. The wind had a bite, but the cold felt refreshing on Mila's hot cheeks.

Too soon, she had to go back inside.

At least by then, the desserts—bone-chip cookies, broomstick brownies, and midnight ice cream—were already being served. Mila skipped them even if broomstick brownies were her favorite.

Soon afterward, the entire family moved to the living room to exchange presents. Mila had gone all out like every year and had bought her relatives thoughtful gifts she knew they would appreciate—a new cauldron for her parents, a rare spell book for Kevin, a set of magical herbs and roots for Juniper, and the new Luna the Lucky Witch Doll that Willow wanted so much.

But not even the expression of unadulterated joy on her niece's face as she opened her present could cheer Mila up.

This would go down as the worst Christmas in the history of lousy holidays, and that was fine. Mila just wanted the day to be over and to forget about the love potion, the arrest, and her family's judgmental stares.

Just then, the doorbell rang, and Mila's heart fluttered in her chest. Could it be Riley already?

And why was her heart fluttering at the idea of Chief Inquisitor King waiting at her door, ready to torment her some more with his unbearably good looks and closed-off personality? Or worse, his unsettling thoughts about her mermaid hair. Well, the beanie should solve that, at least.

She scrambled to her feet and quickly made her way to the door, but her mother beat her to it.

And if Mila didn't know better, she'd

say Mom was swooning at finding the chief inquisitor in all his towering might and scarily sexy dark looks on her doorstep.

"Merry Christmas, Mrs. Bennet," Riley was saying. "Sorry to intrude on your celebration..."

Mila's mom squeaked, she *literally* squeaked, as she replied, "No trouble at all, Chief King. Would you like to come in? Have some dragon scale tea or a toadstool infusion?"

Riley briefly looked over Mrs. Bennet's shoulders right at Mila, and, at the subtle but panicked shake of her head, he unleashed a smile on her mother that Mila was sure would shed a few years off the poor woman's life.

"Thank you, Mrs. Bennet, but I'm afraid I don't have time," Riley said, his tone professional but gentle. "I'm here to pick up Mila."

At the speed of light, Mila was by their side, putting on her coat, scarf, hat, and gloves and kissing her still-stunned mom on both cheeks, saying, "Love you, Mom. Talk soon..."

Mila stepped out into the cold winter air without waiting for a reply, letting out a sigh of relief.

She waved back at her mom and

followed Riley down the already-coated driveway while the snow kept on falling.

About halfway down, he tilted his head at her. "That bad, uh?"

"You have no idea." She couldn't help the wide smile that split her face at seeing him again.

They walked in silence for a few moments, the only sound the muffled crunch of snow under their boots. As they made their way down her parents' street toward his car, Mila stole glances at Riley, and a few times, she caught him staring back at her with an unreadable expression that suited his enigmatic personality perfectly. He looked ruggedly handsome but also weirdly more approachable than he had yesterday. Probably because he wasn't trying to put her in jail and throw out the key like he had the previous night.

When they finally reached the car, Riley opened the door for Mila, his hand hovering over the small of her back as she climbed into the passenger seat, grateful for the warmth it offered. Today he was driving a different car from the official police vehicle they'd rode in yesterday, and Mila couldn't help but notice how impeccably clean and organized his— *personal?*—car was. So neat it looked as if he had just driven it out of the dealership that day.

Riley closed her door and circled to the other side, claiming the driver's seat and making the cabin of the car feel immediately ten times smaller than it had a second before.

Then he put the car into gear, and just like that, they were driving away. At once, he started reciting through The Wizarding Code of Conduct in his head.

Mila chuckled and said, "Please pull over."

Riley glanced sideways at her before training his eyes on the icy road again. "Why?"

"Don't worry, I'm not about to turn you into a toad."

She reached out and squeezed his arm. The gesture was meant to be reassuring. Instead, it caused a tingle to shoot up Mila's arm, and she immediately let go. And if the way Riley was crushing the wheel in his grip, his knuckles almost white, was any indication, he'd felt the spark, too.

Still, he flipped the blinker and parked the car on the side of the road, turning to her expectantly.

Chapter Fourteen

With the Intensity of Hellfire

RILEY

The moment the car stopped moving, Mila Bennet rummaged in her overlarge bag and pulled out a small red gift-bag, handing it to him.

A present? She'd gotten him a Christmas present? Why? He hadn't gotten her anything—the thought to get her something hadn't even crossed his mind. And where had she gone to buy him a present on such short notice? He'd dropped her at her house almost at dawn the previous night. Wait, was the gift a way for her to come on to him—

Mila chuckled. "Oh, gargoyles, you have such a big head. I'm not coming on to you, Chief King. Don't worry, your virtue is safe with me."

It's your *virtue you should worry about.* The thought slipped his treacherous mind before he could censor it, and from the way Mila suddenly blushed, she'd heard it loud and clear.

"Yeah," she confirmed. "Transmission received, over," she joked. "Do us both a favor and open your present." She pointed at the red bag now in his hands. "I assure you, it's a gift for me as much as it is for you."

Riley shrugged, curiosity getting the best of him, and retrieved a black wool beanie from within the bag. He stared at it a little puzzled but was about to put it on when she said, "I've enchanted it."

He immediately lowered the hat and stared at it with renewed suspicion.

"Don't worry," Mila continued. "No unsanctioned magic. It's a simple screening spell, but it should prevent me from hearing most of your thoughts. Put in on," she urged him. "Try it."

Not without a healthy dose of skepticism, Riley put her beanie on.

Mila smiled. "You look cute."

He scowled. "I'm not *cute*."

Mila Bennet rolled her eyes. "All right, Mr. *Not* Cute, now try to think something offensive," she prompted.

"Easy," he said, and then thought, *Why did she have to give me a stupid hat?*

To his surprise, Mila didn't react.

"No comeback?" he asked.

"Nope, the beanie is working. Try again."

The next thought that popped into his head was definitely not something he wanted Mila to hear. But he had to test the beanie's enchantment, didn't he? So he thought, *I wonder what she'd sound like moaning my name.*

He waited for Mila's reaction, but once again, there was none. Relief washed over him, and he smiled.

"See?" She beamed back at him and affectionally punched him in the arm. "The beanie rules. Now, one last test. Think something a little more risqué."

Riley smirked. "I think we're good."

Mila's eyes widened. "Why? Was your last thought dirty? What did you think?"

Riley was ecstatic at having the privacy of his thoughts back and couldn't resist teasing her a little. "You'd like to know, wouldn't you?"

"I'm not so sure." She pouted. "But at least we know the beanie works."

And just as well, given how much that pout made him want to kiss her. It was a pull so strong it scared him.

Mila reared her head back, and Riley scowled. "Wait, did you hear that?"

"Not exactly." She studied him for a long moment. "But I got a sense of the emotion behind the thought. The beanie doesn't work if you go too intense on me, Chief King."

"Noted," he said, then thought, *and*

she'd better stop calling me Chief King.

The appellative on her lips had switched from a perceived mockery to a turn on.

Mila didn't react, and Riley sighed with relief in his head once again. The beanie wasn't perfect, but at least it kept *most* of his inappropriate thoughts private.

All he had to do now was to stop wanting to kiss the witch next to him with the intensity of hellfire, and he'd be good.

Riley put the car into gear and once again merged into the non-existent traffic.

Chapter Fifteen

Between a Rock and a Hard Mattress

MILA

Mila was conscious the beanie had been her idea and that it was best for Riley and her to keep out of each other's heads.

But right now, as she watched his inscrutable expression as he drove on through the winter storm, she couldn't help the burning desire to know exactly what he was thinking.

Was it about her? Or was he concentrated on solving the case?

"You're staring," he called out, making her jump in her seat.

"I'm sorry, the silence is weird." Then, to move the conversation along, she added, "Where are we going?"

"I thought we'd hit the hospital first to see if Mrs. Blackwell has made any progress."

"Oh, all right."

And just like that, they were plunged back into silence.

Mila tried to stifle a yawn, but it escaped her lips before she could. She felt

Riley's gaze on her and looked back at him sheepishly.

"Sorry," she said.

"Don't be." Riley's voice was low and rough, sending shivers down her spine. "Yesterday was a long night."

"You probably think I'm an ungrateful brat," she said, feeling embarrassed.

Riley turned to her briefly with a questioning look etched between his brows. "Why would I think that?"

She blushed a little as she said the next part. "My familiar told me you gave me the entire time-stretch pill, so I've had at least four more hours of sleep than you, and yet here I am in your car yawning like a lazy house cat."

Silence stretched between them again until Mila broke it. "Thank you, by the way, for the pill and for carrying me to bed last night."

Riley didn't respond immediately, so much so that Mila began to think he hadn't heard her. But then his eyes flickered briefly to hers before he focused back on the road. "It's no problem."

He took a sharp right turn, and they arrived at the hospital. Well, at least the most awkward car ride in the history of awkward car rides was over, Mila thought to herself as Riley backed into a parallel parking spot. The maneuver took him all of ten seconds, while it would've taken Mila at least fifteen tries, a lot of sweat, and even more cursing.

Not going to lie. The way he drove was sexy as hell.

Mila's thoughts cooled off the moment they stepped out of the car and an icy wind assaulted them. She pulled her coat closer to herself and followed Riley inside the hospital—a large, imposing building, with its lights casting an eerie glow on the surrounding area.

They were at a regular human hospital. Since Mrs. Blackwell was human and the poison she'd ingested natural, the magimedics had deferred her here.

The receptionist at the front desk gave them directions to Mrs. Blackwell's room, and they made their way down the hallway and up two floors.

Just as they were approaching the room, they spotted an old couple coming out of it.

Riley, projecting all his big-bad-cop aura, stopped them. "Are you friends of Mrs. Blackwell?"

He wasn't wearing a uniform today, but somehow the two humans immediately picked up on the fact that he was law enforcement.

"Yes, Detective," the frail old woman replied. "We all play Buraco in the same club." Then she patted the arm of her companion. "George and I didn't want Josephine to spend Christmas alone. Pity she hasn't woken up yet. Awful thing, what happened to her, really awful."

"How did you know she was at the hospital?" Riley asked, ever the suspicious cop.

"Oh, we were there last night when it happened," the wiry old man replied. He had sad blue eyes and his voice quivered slightly. "All our grandkids go to the same school."

Riley extracted a small notebook from his pocket. "May I have your names, please?"

Mila rolled her eyes. These two looked pathetically harmless.

"Sure," both the elderlies said and proceeded to give Riley their generalities.

"I'm Cherry Knox," the woman said. "And my nephew is Peter Knox."

When it was the man's turn, he sighed pitifully before saying, "George Harrison MacNeil and my granddaughter is Judy MacNeil."

Riley thanked them, and after a quick goodbye nod, the couple ambled down the hall toward the elevator.

"You seriously think those two had something to do with the murder attempt?" Mila hissed once the couple was out of earshot.

"Most killers are notorious for coming back to the scene of the crime, especially if they didn't finish the job on the first attempt," he said, and without a second glance her way, Riley went ahead into Mrs. Blackwell's room.

A nurse was stationed there, and from the subtle nod she and Riley exchanged, she must've been one of theirs, an undercover agent from the Department of Magical Justice. She had a sleek bob of black-blue hair, warm brown eyes, and slightly bronzed skin with a warm, golden undertone. In summer, Mila would've assumed she was tanned, but since it was the dead of winter, that must be her natural skin tone.

"Any progress here?" Riley asked in a voice of authority that landed like a ball of fire straight into Mila's core.

If he used that voice on her, she'd let him handcuff her to the bed—or any other piece of furniture, really—whenever he wanted.

The nurse shook her head. "No change, Inquisitor King." Her words confirmed she was DMJ. "Mrs. Blackwell is still in a pharmacologically induced coma."

Riley approached the bed, looking down at the pale figure lying there. Mila followed him, and if what Abel had claimed in court to get her released was true—that her love potion had saved this woman's life, Mila didn't feel so sorry anymore about the mess she'd made. Yeah, she'd been arrested, humiliated, and had spent Christmas Eve stuck in a gym with strangers. She'd become the family weirdo, the neighborhood laughing stock, and on top of that, she was stuck doing community service with the most unsettling man on the planet.

But looking at Mrs. Blackwell's almost serene face in her pharmacological sleep, Mila decided it had all been worth it if her potion had really saved this poor woman's life.

"Did the doctors say when they plan on waking her up?" Riley asked the fake nurse, wrenching Mila out of her thoughts.

"It could still be a couple of days," the nurse responded. "They're not sure."

"All right, Agent Callidora. Keep up the good work and thank you for sticking it out on Christmas. Olympia will be here soon to take over, so you'll get at least to taste some bone-chips cookies with your family."

"Thank you, Chief."

"Don't mention it."

Then Chief Inquisitor Riley King did the unthinkable and winked at the nurse, who crossed her eyes and made a funny face back.

Mila stared at him in horror because, if seeing his gorgeous but unattainable side was unsettling, watching him be kind to his colleagues, joke around, and playfully wink at random nurses was dangerous on a whole other level. Especially since he'd made it clear that even if seeing her naked in the tub might've elicited some unwanted sexual fantasies, he was not interested in pursuing something romantic with her.

He basically had a sign on his chest stapled over his heart that said: *Keep out! Trespassers will be shot on sight.*

"So, what's next?" Mila asked as they exited the room.

"I thought we could go back to the station, bounce ideas off each other for potential leads. You said last night you had a few suspects?"

"Yeah, I do." And she wanted to share her theories with him, but just the idea of going back to the police station where she'd been dragged to handcuffed and wearing only a pink bathrobe and feathery slippers no later than last night made her feel gross all over again.

"Something the matter?" Riley asked, probably picking up on her discomfort.

"Yeah, could we *not* go to the police station?"

Riley studied her while they waited for the elevator, his head tilted to the side. He smiled down at her, and his words were kind rather than teasing as he said, "Mug shot still too fresh in your mind?"

For no apparent logical reason, her heart fluttered in her chest and her mouth went dry, so she just nodded.

"All right, Bennet, where do you want to go?"

Her stomach grumbled in response.

Riley's smile widened. "Skipped on the grand meal today?"

Mila nodded. "I didn't have much of an appetite."

"Glad to see that's changed." Riley deployed the wink on her, wreaking all kinds of havoc in her already grumbling stomach. "What do you say we get Chinese take-out and then get back to mine to discuss the case?"

"Yeah, sure," Mila squeaked, thinking this was the Cosmo's revenge for the way she'd mentally teased her mother for squeaking in the same way.

"Great." He flashed her another stomach-melting grin. "I know just the place."

The entire way to the car, then to the Chinese restaurant, and finally to Riley's house, Mila kept her raging thoughts in check by repeating to herself a string of steadying reassurances: *he's not taking you back to his place to ravage you. He probably isn't even interested in kissing you. He only wants to discuss the case in a private space, not test his new rock-hard mattress with you, definitely not test his new rock-hard mattress with you...*

Mmm, I wonder what else he has that's rock hard...

No, no, no, no... bad Mila, we're not interested in anything rock hard that Chief Riley King might have to offer.

Aren't we?

Nope, one hundred percent not.

Mental sigh. If only he didn't smell like stardust and temptation. Having spent an unhealthy amount of time in his arms, or stuck in the front seat of a car with him, the scent was ingrained in her brain.

At least now, the Chinese food they were taking to his house covered some of it and, oh, look, they were pulling over...

Chapter Sixteen

Drama about a Drama

RILEY

If the concept of eating Chinese take-out on Christmas evening after having spent half the day working wasn't at all extraneous to Riley, doing it at his place with a gorgeous witch he had an undeniable attraction to was definitely new.

He observed Mila Bennet as she enthusiastically removed all the containers from the take-out bags and lined them on his coffee table.

They were in his living room, sitting on the floor in front of the fireplace that he had magically lit the moment they'd stepped into the house.

And the scene was starting to look a little *too* cozy. Better to remind everyone—himself included—that they were here to work.

But seeing how Mila was clearly famished, he let her have a few bites before discussing the case. Meanwhile, Riley did his best to ignore the little noises of appreciation that escaped her mouth as she chewed, or how her plush lips contorted in pleasure. But golems be dammed, he couldn't help wondering how all those little sounds would translate between the sheets.

His only saving grace was the beanie still firmly stuck over his head. He would never remove it, not indoors, and not even to go to bed.

Once Mila had scarfed down two entire containers of food, he finally broached the subject they were here to discuss. "What was it you discovered last night?"

Her tongue darted between her lips to lick the sauce out the corner of her mouth in a way that was too distracting for anyone's good, then she wiped herself with a napkin and finally responded. "Oh, right, so you know I had to administer the antidote to all the people who'd eaten my loved-up cupcakes."

He nodded.

"Well, I had to stay with each of my..." Mila paused, probably searching for the right word.

"Victims?" Riley offered with a smirk.

She threw a fortune cookie at him. "I was going to say *patients* for at least twenty minutes afterward, listening to all their woes. And while most of it was lovesick gibberish, I also gleaned some interesting facts."

Riley raised an eyebrow. "Such as?"

Even if they were alone in the house, Mila spoke in hushed tones next, "The mom of one of Willow's schoolmates told me that before the recital started, Mrs. Blackwell got into a heated argument with another mom."

Riley dropped his chopstick and focused all his attention on Mila. "Whose mom and about what?"

"The altercation was with Macie Princeton. From what my sister has told me about Willow's classmates and their families, she's one of those hyper soccer moms whose entire life revolves around proving her child is better than anyone else's. And she was mad at Mrs. Blackwell because her daughter hadn't gotten the principal role in the recital."

Riley waited for the rest. "And?"

"And nothing, that's it."

"You think a kid not getting the principal role in an *elementary school* recital is reason enough to murder the drama teacher?"

Mila shrugged. "I don't know. Is there ever a good reason to kill someone? And at least we know of a suspect who had a clear grudge against the victim."

Riley shoved the empty take-out

containers aside and replaced them with the case files, quickly shuffling through them. "Yeah, several people reported the fight between Mrs. Blackwell and Mrs. Princeton, so at least it was loud enough that many people heard it."

"Did Macie Princeton give a justification in her statement?" Mila asked.

"Let's check." Riley shuffled through all the depositions, once, twice, and then looked up at Mila. "That's odd."

"What?"

"I don't have a statement from Mrs. Princeton."

"Oh, I thought all people present had been deposed."

"They have, which means either Mrs. Princeton had already left or..."

"She didn't want to be deposed," Mila finished the sentence for him.

Look at them already finishing each other's sentences. Riley ground his teeth. *No, nope, not going there, back to the case.*

"Would that even have been possible with all the magical law enforcers around for her to have escaped?" Mila continued.

Riley shrugged. "The school is big. If someone really wanted to avoid detection, they could've easily found a hiding spot."

He took the file with the name and address of Macie Princeton and set it aside. "I think Mrs. Princeton has earned a visit from us. Good job. What else have you got, Bennet?"

 # Chapter Seventeen

We Shouldn't Be Doing This

MILA

Riley using her surname shouldn't have sounded sexy. It wasn't even particularly intimate. To the contrary, it was probably a custom among colleagues in the magical force to call each other by their surnames, as opposed to using first names.

And Riley had simply said, good job. Not something like "what an exemplary piece of investigative work you did" or something.

But that didn't hinder the warm glow that spread through Mila at the objectively lackluster praise.

She reined in the excessive swooning and concentrated on giving him an answer. "My next suspect is Mrs. Blackwell's grandson."

Riley shuffled the case files again with that deliciously sexy frown etched between his brows. "I thought it odd, too, that a twenty-eight-year-old man would spend his evening at an elementary school recital just because his grandmother is the drama teacher."

"Yeah, but the janitor, after he was sane enough to stop babbling about being in love with the school's nurse for five minutes, told me that Mrs. Blackwell is secretly loaded, like in she's stinking rich."

"Why would a rich person work at an elementary school?"

Mila waved him off. "Rumor has it a love of drama, both on and off stage, and plain, old boredom. Anyway, apparently her grandson is the biggest suck-up and has been her puppet ever since she wrote him in her will as her principal heir."

"And you think he might've killed her to speed up the inheritance process. Checks out." Riley moved another file on top of that of Mrs. Princeton. "Trent Blackwell has also gained a visit from us. Who's your last suspect? You had three, right?"

Mila absentmindedly grabbed a fortune cookie and was about to unwrap it when Riley reached out and blocked her hand with his. "Don't."

Mila stared down at their joined hands, her heart thudding in her chest. She felt the heat of Riley's hand through her own, and the sensation was far from unpleasant.

"Sorry," he said, retreating his hand and its warmth.

"Why don't you want me to open the fortune cookie?"

"I don't trust the accuracy of their predictions."

Mila laughed. "Come on, it's just a fortune cookie. I promise not to take whatever pearl of wisdom is contained inside too much to heart." She unwrapped the cookie, broke it in half, and read the message hidden within:

Sometimes love is staring you right in the face.

She swallowed, looked up at the gorgeous man who, at the moment, was very much staring her in the face, and dropped the tiny sheet of paper as if it had burned her.

Riley raised an eyebrow. "What did it say?"

"Nothing, you're right. These things are silly. But how come you're such a fortune cookie hater?"

Riley smiled and shrugged in a self-deprecatory way. "Guess my mom has always been against sub-standard future telling."

"Your mom?" Mila frowned, then she put two and two together. Her brain cross-referenced his surname with that of famous seers, and she gasped. "Your mom is Glenda King? *The* Glenda King?"

Riley gave her a tiny nod.

"Gargoyles, you must introduce me. I've always wanted to have a reading with her, but her waitlist is like, insane."

"Yeah, right," Riley scoffed.

Mila scowled. "Why? You think your mom wouldn't like me?"

Riley nailed her with such a penetrating stare that Mila felt like he was looking directly into her soul. "No, Mila, she'd probably like you too much."

He'd called her Mila. And now, the way her name sounded on his lips, rolled out in a lush whisper that had the power to melt glaciers, to resuscitate the dead, to make the sun rise at midnight, would be forever etched in her memory.

Riley visibly regretted the words the moment they left his mouth because next, he added, "Anyway, forget about my mom. It's getting late and we should wrap this up."

Mila felt a pang of disappointment but tried to shake it off, nodding in agreement. She followed his this-is-just-a-professional-consultation lead and went back to discussing the case. "The last lead I have is that Mrs. Blackwell's former lover was also present at the recital. Another grandma in their Buraco club gossiped that Mrs. Blackwell had recently broken up with him. And while the official reason had been that the relationship had run its course, the dumped gentleman is convinced she's already involved with someone else."

"All right, but why would a former lover try to murder her if he still had feelings? Shouldn't he go after the other man?"

"Perhaps, but what if he couldn't find out who it was or if his approach was more a case of"—Mila made a silly dude voice—"If I can't have her, no one will."

Riley chuckled at that, but still scratched his temple, unconvinced. "I don't know. Passion crimes are usually more impulsive. Poisoning someone is a cold, premeditated act. It doesn't really fit the MO of a crime of passion." Still, he reached for the file of the scorned lover and put it on top of the pile with the other two suspects. "But still worth digging a little deeper into."

As he finished talking, Mila realized she'd been fixating on his mouth. His full lips had her deeply hypnotized. But now that they'd stopped moving, her gaze snapped up to meet the dark wall of his obsidian eyes.

He arched an eyebrow, asking a question she didn't know how to answer. So, for lack of better alternatives, she got up and fled, pretending to need the bathroom—very much her MO today. Only this wasn't her house, and she had no idea where she was going.

Mila sensed Riley standing behind her before he even spoke. "Bathroom is the second door down the hall." The words came out in a dangerously low rumble.

Mila turned and suddenly realized they were standing in a very narrow, very dark hallway with a mere two inches of space separating them.

Their eyes met, and Mila's heart leaped, racing out of control. She couldn't help but stare into the inky pools of his eyes, drawn like a moth toward a flame.

Riley's gaze flickered down to her lips and quickly back up. The tension between them was palpable. She licked her lips nervously, and Riley's pupils dilated.

Her heart was pounding in her chest. They were so close that she could see the tiny flecks of silver hidden within the black of his intense gaze. She could feel the heat of his body emanating from him, making her feel dizzy and disorientated.

She tried to speak, but suddenly her throat was dry and no words would come out.

Riley took a step closer, his body pressing up against hers as he whispered in her ear, "You know we shouldn't be doing this, right?"

Mila bit her bottom lip and nodded slowly. But she couldn't deny the fact that her body was screaming for more. She wanted his touch, his kiss, his everything. It was like they were two magnets being drawn together.

He reached out and brushed a strand of hair from her face before cupping her cheek in his hand. His thumb stroked over her lips in a teasing motion before he leaned in and pressed his mouth against hers.

Mila's knees almost buckled beneath her at the feel of his lips moving softly against hers. She could taste the sweetness of the bubble tea he'd been drinking on his breath as he deepened the kiss, wrapping his arm around her waist as he pulled her flush against him.

Time stopped, they stood frozen in an alternative dimension, lost in their own little world where nothing else mattered except for each other.

And things got a lot worse as Mila reached up and pulled the beanie off of him. She wanted to hear all of him, needed to feel both his body and his mind pressed against her.

Chapter Eighteen

Not Passion, Not Desire, and Most Certainly Not Love

MILA

The second Mila removed the beanie, Riley's emotions slammed into her like a tidal wave. His thoughts weren't spelled out in coherent phrases she could hear or read, but they were strong enough to decipher easily.

He wanted her; he wanted her just as much as she wanted him. Mila grabbed onto his shoulders and let her thoughts flow unguarded, responding to his avalanche of raw emotions and desires with equal force.

She could tell the moment Riley felt it from the way he intensified the kiss, if that was even possible.

His hands traveled down to the small of her back, pressing her closer to him as they kissed with reckless abandon. Mila moaned softly against his lips as their electric chemistry, palpable and all-consuming, coursed through her body.

Riley's deft fingers were drawing circles on the small of her back, causing every nerve ending on her body to feel so damn good it almost hurt. Mila responded eagerly, tangling her fingers into his hair and pulling him even closer until she could feel every single one of his hard muscles pressed against her. And it still wasn't enough.

Riley must've come to the same conclusion because, with an animalistic growl, he pushed her backward until her back hit the wall. Then he was on her, caging her between the hard wall and his even harder body, and there was no more space left between them.

But even that didn't last. Without a word, Riley scooped her up into his powerful arms and carried her down the hall to the bedroom, where he gently laid her on the bed. It looked like they *were* going to test the hard mattress after all.

The sheets were cool against what little skin her winter clothes left exposed. But as Riley climbed on top of her, the cool sheets became the last of her worries.

Mila arched her back to meet his body in mid-air as Riley's mouth claimed hers once more, his hands roaming over her with a desperate hunger that left her trembling with need.

It was like they couldn't get close

enough to each other, like no matter how hard they pressed against each other, it'd never be enough. More, she needed, more. The craving was so powerful it almost felt wrong.

But then Riley kissed her neck. He sucked her earlobe, grazing it with just the right amount of teeth to send a shiver of pleasure coursing down her spine, and her recriminations almost melted away. Mila was about to let herself go completely, to forget about reason and just give in to her desire when Riley lifted his head and looked at her. And that's when Mila recognized the speckles of silver in his eyes for what they really were. Not passion, not desire, and most certainly not love.

It was magic. *Her* magic.

Chapter Nineteen

You've Nothing to Be Sorry About

RILEY

One moment Riley was passionately kissing Mila on his bed, and the next, he was being flung off her with preternatural force.

He landed on the opposite side of the mattress, momentarily confused, and then looked up at Mila, who had already hopped off the bed and was pacing his bedroom, visibly shaken.

He was a complete and total troll.

Riley sat on the side of the bed closer to her and did the only logical thing, apologize for his unforgivable behavior. "I'm sorry," he said. "I thought you wanted this too, but I obviously got carried away."

Mila's reaction was once again not what he'd expected. She crossed the room in two quick steps, planted a hand over his mouth, and eyes blazing, she told him, "You have nothing to apologize for. I'm the one to blame here."

Riley raised an eyebrow, and since she was still blocking his mouth, he sent her his rebuff mind to mind. *"I'm pretty sure I was part of that, too."*

Mila's eyebrows drooped, and she looked like she was on the verge of tears. "Only because you had no choice."

Next, she ran back down the hall just as unexpectedly and returned to the bedroom, carrying the black beanie she'd removed earlier.

She secured the hat back on his head, saying, "Sorry, but I don't think I can handle hearing your reaction to what I'm about to tell you."

Okay, now he was seriously freaked out. But he let her have a minute to straighten her thoughts, since she was clearly upset.

"It's the love potion," Mila finally blurted. "Last night, I ate the cupcake, went to take a bath, and when I woke up, I was in your arms."

Riley frowned, still unsure of what she was getting at.

"Don't you get it? You're the first man I saw. This weird attraction that you don't seem to be able to fight, despite wanting to... you *can't* because of the love potion. I heard your thoughts yesterday. You literally like me against your will. You don't really find me attractive. You don't want to kiss me or do other..." She blushed. "*Stuff*... The enchantment of the love potion is forcing you to."

Oh, Mila, she really knew nothing. Riley had felt the magic between them, too, but it had nothing to do with her love potion. And he was pretty sure he *wanted* to kiss her and do other *stuff* to her, *with* her. Many unholy things. But that didn't mean he should.

Riley forced the untruth of what she was saying in a corner so dark and remote of his soul that even he wouldn't be able to reach it anymore.

Kissing her had changed everything. He had a strong suspicion now on why they shared a mental bond without needing to consult his mother's spell book. A kiss like that—yeah, it was enough to know.

But dating a cop was no life. He'd seen the years of worry tear down at his mother until that faithful night when all her worst fears had come true. Glenda had never recovered from the loss of his father, who had been the previous Chief Inquisitor. And Riley wouldn't want to bestow such a fate on anyone, least of all gentle, funny, sparkly Mila Bennet.

So he went along with what she was saying. "Can you make more antidote?"

"Too late," she responded as he knew

she would. "The magic has settled in."

He watched her pace his bedroom, expression riddled with guilt, and felt like a total dirtbag for keeping her in the dark. But it was the best thing to do, especially for her.

She stopped and turned to him. "I'm so sorry this happened. I wish I'd never made that potion. No, I mean, it's good that I did. Otherwise, Mrs. Blackwell would be dead. But I'm sorry for what"— she circled a hand in his general direction—"it's doing to you. I'm so sorry for that."

Riley couldn't take her misplaced guilt anymore so, even if probably it wasn't the best move, he stood up and pulled her into his arms. "You've nothing to be sorry about. I shouldn't have kissed you. It won't happen again."

Chapter Twenty

Magically Induced or Not, Unrequited Love Sucks

MILA

Riley was taking the news that he'd been cursed into loving her fairly well. Which was good. And he was also saying he wouldn't kiss her again. Also a good thing, probably for the best.

Technically, *theoretically,* because right now, as he gently circled his palm over her back in a soothing gesture, all Mila wanted to do was tilt her chin up and pick up where they'd left off on the bed not five minutes ago.

Or at least the influence of the love potion wanted her to. Right. This feeling, this craving that had been building inside her, wasn't real. It was magic. The byproduct of an incantation she shouldn't have used to influence somebody else's emotions and her own. Suddenly, all her father's cautionary tales about the unethical misuse of magic made total sense.

When she'd brewed the potion, Mila had thought she'd give herself a meet cute, and instead, she'd scrambled with the Chief Inquisitor's heart and her own.

"It's getting late," Riley said, in that low tone of his that now had become torture to hear. "I should take you home."

The low caress of his voice grated against her heart like a blade. His scent, his voice, his body, his heart, all things she could almost touch but never have, not now that everything had been tainted by her stupid potion.

Her feelings felt real, but she'd never taken a love potion before, so she had no way of assessing how love enchantments worked, how good they were at making feelings that weren't really there feel real. Whatever she had with Riley would forever be tainted by doubt, by the shadow of her spellwork. Even if they somehow decided to ignore the facts, she could never fully trust anything they'd build. And so, as hard as it was and contrary to every last one of her instincts, she pulled away from him, putting a healthy amount of physical distance between them.

"Actually, can you bring me to the station?"

Riley frowned. "To the station, why?"

"My broomstick is still impounded. I'd like to get it back."

He stared out the dark windows where the wind could be heard howling between the tree branches. Snow was still falling. "There's a storm outside. You're not flying in this weather."

Right now, she wanted nothing more than to fly right at the center of a storm, but Riley's tone was so final she knew there'd be no point in arguing with him.

"Come on, let's go. I'll take you home."

She nodded.

They moved back into the living room. Mila, taking in the mess of discarded take-out boxes, offered to help him clean up.

"Leave it," Riley said. "I'll take care of it tomorrow."

Guess he couldn't wait to be rid of her. And how to blame him? If someone had bewitched her, she'd feel the same.

He grabbed a thick, brown wool coat from the closet and he put it on while she did the same with her red one.

Outside, the snow was falling thick and fast.

Riley turned up his collar, and they walked to his car, the windshield already covered by a thick white blanket. A snap of his fingers, and it was gone.

Ever the gentleman, he circled to her side of the car first and held the door open for her. She slipped in, noticing that he didn't shut the door right away, and she caught him studying her face through the reflection of the window as if he were memorizing her features. Dread twisted inside of her.

Magically induced or not, unrequited love felt awful. She hoped Riley wasn't experiencing the same intense misery. Mila couldn't bear to have inflicted such suffering on another person.

Riley closed the door and got in from the driver's side. The proximity of sharing a car felt suddenly unbearable. Then they were moving.

The ride to her house was a quiet one.

She turned her gaze toward the window, to the night outside, watching the snow swirl around and tumble down the glass.

They were already on her street when he finally broke the silence. "I should probably pick you up early tomorrow if we want to interrogate all three suspects," he said. "Eight o'clock?"

Right. Because they were still stuck together until the murder case was solved. For a second, Mila hated the professional detachment of his words. Despised it with every fiber in her soul.

But what other choice did they have if

not to distance themselves?

She sighed, feeling a lump form in her throat. "Yeah, eight sounds good."

Riley pulled up to the curb and parked. They sat in silence for a moment, staring straight ahead, the only sound the whistling wind outside. At least she hoped he couldn't hear the disappointed pounding of her heart in her chest.

"Well," he said finally. "Goodnight, Mila."

"Goodnight, Riley." She opened the door and stepped out into the snow, her heart heavy.

Mila ran up her driveway. She let herself in, and keeping shelter behind a curtain, watched his car still parked outside. It was a few long minutes before he drove away.

Only when the taillights of Riley's car disappeared down the road, did Mila let herself cry.

 Chapter Twenty-one

That's Just Hysterical

RILEY

After dropping Mila off, Riley drove himself home, his fingers curled around the wheel like talons, digging into the leather to avoid punching something.

He felt like the worst kind of ghoul for deceiving her. Riley hadn't exactly lied, but he had omitted the truth and now he'd have to live with the consequences.

He parked his car in the driveway and sat for a moment, still clutching the steering wheel, still hating himself. Riley lay his head backward against the headrest and closed his eyes, taking a moment to remember how kissing Mila had felt. Magical, exhilarating, *real.* The way she'd tasted, the way she'd felt pressed against his chest, the little noises she'd made.

Good thing they hadn't gone any further than kissing, or Riley wasn't sure he'd have had the strength to do what needed to be done. Not that keeping away from Mila was going to be any easier as things stood.

Riley sat there in his car in the cold, alternatively regretting what he'd done and then convincing himself it had been the right choice. These thoughts circled over his heart and brain, their contrasting reasonings an endless loop that was threatening to drive him insane.

Right decision or not, Riley punched the wheel in frustration and finally got out of the car, trudging through the snow to his front door. The moment he stepped inside the house, he was greeted by the smell of the Chinese food they'd eaten that still clung to the air and the faint smoke of the dying embers in the fireplace.

The smells were no bother. They could be easily dispelled. He opened a window and the frigid winter wind took care of purging the air in a few minutes.

But the silence that greeted him was almost suffocating.

After tossing his keys on the kitchen counter, Riley ignored the carton boxes a while longer and went into his study to retrieve the magical tome he'd borrowed from his mother's library earlier that day.

He sat at his desk and opened the book, flipping the pages until he reached the section on the possible reasons why unrelated witches might experience mental bonds.

Being under the influence of a shared spell was a prominent one. Good, that would only reinforce Mila's theory if she did some research.

But that wasn't what he was looking for. Riley kept reading until he reached the passage that interested him and which confirmed his worst fears.

He snapped the book shut. No matter what the fine print said, he and Mila couldn't be together. It was for her own good.

Riley threw the book into a drawer where it landed with a heavy thud. In a fit of frustration, he slammed the drawer shut and locked it, out of sight, out of mind. Then he went to the living room to clear out the take-out boxes. On his third trip to the bin, a tiny slip of paper caught his attention. It was the message Mila had found inside the fortune cookie and had refused to share with him.

Riley picked it up from the floor and read it.

Sometimes love is staring you right in the face.

Oh, that was just hysterical. So much for Glenda's mistrust of fortune cookies. Apparently, they were spot on.

Pity it wasn't meant to be.

Riley crunched the tiny slip of paper in his fist and then threw it on the dying embers in the fireplace.

The paper twisted, darkened, and soon caught fire, disappearing in a blink just like his future with Mila had.

 ## Chapter Twenty-two

That's Going to Be So Much Fun

MILA

"Are you crying?" Abel asked in a concerned voice as he brushed against her legs.

"No," Mila sobbed. She bent to pick him up and nuzzled his head.

"Okay, so is that dew streaming down your cheeks?"

"Maybe I'm crying a little bit."

Abel sighed. "So, you figured it out."

"Figured out what?"

"About the love potion."

Indignant, Mila dropped Abel on the kitchen counter. "You knew?"

"I had a suspicion."

"Why didn't you tell me anything?"

"I tried to this morning, but you were in a hurry to leave and I didn't think the magic would act so swiftly or wreak so much damage already."

"Oh, it's nothing. I'm not damaged on top of desperate. Don't worry." To distract herself, Mila put the kettle on. She could use a little moonlight tea to ease the nerves.

Abel trotted over to her, following the U-shape of the kitchen until he reached the stove. "I wasn't saying you were damaged, but clearly, you're upset. Did something happen with Inquisitor King?"

Mila shrugged. "We kissed, and it was magical... but of course, it wasn't *real*. Just part of the love potion enchantment."

Abel bumped his head against her arm, repeating, "I'm sorry."

She scratched his chin. "It's not your fault. You tried to warn me not to brew a love potion. I'm the one who didn't listen."

The kettle whistled, and Mila took it off the stove. She poured the hot water into a mug and added a spoon of moonlight dust.

They moved to the couch, Mila sipping her tea and absentmindedly stroking Abby as he curled in her lap.

"Do you know of a way to make the magic wear off faster when it is too late to take an antidote?"

Abel made biscuits on her legs. "I did a little research this morning. The only valid suggestion I found is to stay as far away from the object of your affection as you can."

Mila chortled at that. "Fat chance of that happening since we're bound to solve this case together by a magical sentence."

Abel stopped purring long enough to say, "Then maybe you should petition Judge Templeton to commute your sentence to a different public service." The cat yawned. "She seemed like a reasonable woman. If you explain the situation to her, she won't want to force you to spend time with Chief King knowing what we've learned."

"Actually, you're right." Mila dropped her mug onto the coffee table and slid out from under the cat.

She retrieved her laptop from her bedroom and went back to the couch to log on to The Department of Magical Justice website on the darknet, the shadow computer network that was accessible only to witches and wizards.

Judge Templeton had no appointments available the next day. She was probably still off for the holidays, but she had a free late-evening slot on the 27th.

Mila let the cursor hover over the button to book the appointment. If she did talk to the judge, it was probable that afterward, she'd never see Riley again. Yeah, Salem was a small town, but she hadn't met Riley in twenty-nine years and unless she planned on getting arrested on the regular—which she didn't—they probably wouldn't cross paths that often, if ever.

The prospect was heartbreaking. But what was the alternative? The attraction she was feeling toward him was too fast and furious to be real. They'd known each other barely a day. She couldn't be in love with him. The way she was feeling was the potion's doing. And if the only known cure was not to see him, the sooner she started, the sooner she'd heal.

Mila clicked on the calendar, input her credentials, and locked in the appointment. Then she got ready for bed and cried herself to sleep.

***

The next morning, she was ready well before eight. No matter that she'd decided she wasn't going to see Riley ever again after tomorrow. That didn't mean she couldn't look at least presentable for the last two days they had to spend together.

So she'd gotten up at the crack of dawn to get ready, not that it'd been an effort. Her struggling heart had woken her up with its stilted, painful tempo at six o'clock.

Mila had showered, blow-dried her long hair, and tried her best to keep her makeup subtle but sophisticated. Then, she'd spent a good hour in front of her closet, trying to pick the perfect detective outfit that would be contextually flattering but not too sexy, and professional but still look approachable. She'd landed on a striped wool dress in black and purple. Definitely not intimidating.

In her short time as a private investigator, she'd found people were more prone to be forthcoming if they felt like they could trust you. Scare tactics had never proven a good strategy.

Breakfast had been next. But by the time Riley rang the doorbell, she'd already been sitting on her couch, staring at the front door restlessly for over twenty minutes.

She took a deep breath and put on a brave face as she went to open the door. But nothing could've prepared her for the sight of Chief Inquisitor Riley King standing on her doorstep in all his tallish handsomeness.

He was wearing her beanie, the long, heavy coat from last night, and a smile that could melt the snow off the entire neighborhood. He was simply irresistible and equally off-limits.

Mila tried to rein in her emotions and failed spectacularly as she greeted him with a simple, "Hi," that came out more like a strangled whisper.

Riley kept smiling at her, tilting his head. "Nice outfit," he said, pointing to her striped sheath dress. "*Very* subtle on the witching thing."

Despite the teasing, Mila smiled. At least *one* of them could keep their cool and act normal.

"I was going for approachable." She cleared her throat and took a step back to let him in while she put on her winter gear.

Riley stepped into her apartment and waited patiently for her to get ready.

"Chief King." Abel sauntered into the hall, displaying a healthy amount of male territoriality.

"Ah, Pawington the III, Esquire. Good to see you again."

Mila rolled her eyes at the not-so-subtle display of polite hostility and cut it short before it could escalate. "I'm ready."

Mila crouched to the floor to kiss Abel goodbye and then stepped onto the porch, waiting for Riley to get out as well before locking the door.

As she turned, she found him

standing behind her, one arm lifted, offering her a paper cup. He was, in fact, holding a cup in each hand. She'd been so busy admiring his perfect, rugged, sexy face that she hadn't even noticed the cups until now.

"I brought you a Potentilla Latte," he said. "I thought we might both use one after last night."

He was being excruciatingly nice. Mila took the latte only saying, "Thanks."

But as they walked down her driveway, he bumped shoulders with her. "Come on, just because we can't kiss, it doesn't mean we can't be friends."

Okay, so at least they weren't avoiding the elephant in the room—or in the front yard—or being awkward about it. That wrenched the first genuine smile out of her since the previous night.

"Or I could still turn you into a toad and solve all my problems."

The smile he flashed her in response was devastating. "I thought we'd settled on a sea turd."

And now she was outright guffawing, an undignified sound that raised straight from her belly. "Careful what you wish for, Chief King."

Ah, as if *she* could talk. Wishing for a tall, handsome stranger to sweep her off her feet was exactly what had landed her into this mess. Mila sipped on her latte and tried not to think about how it tasted like forbidden love. Or how the warmth of the cup in her hands was nothing compared to the heat Riley's hands had seared into her skin the previous night. Darn potion.

None of this is real, she repeated to herself for the millionth time since last night.

With that thought clear in her mind, she walked the rest of the way to Riley's car and got herself inside before he could hold the door open for her. From now on, they were officially colleagues only. He didn't need to fuss over her.

"I could've gotten the door for you," Riley said as he settled into the driver's seat.

"Would you have gotten the door for another of your agents?"

Riley didn't reply, meaning no.

"Then, I'm good," Mila concluded, taking another sip of delicious latte.

Riley rolled his eyes, and even if she couldn't hear his thoughts, the gesture clearly read, *women!* Either that generalization or an *impossible woman* aimed directly at her.

"Men are equally impossible," Mila

rebuffed.

Riley startled, checking the beanie was properly placed over his head, which made Mila laugh.

"Don't worry, I didn't need to read your thoughts to know what you were thanking."

"Miss Bennet, I see you're a firecracker right from the morrow."

Thank gargoyles he hadn't called her Mila. Just the memory of her name on his lips was enough to make her toes curl and her heart shatter a little.

Still, Mila collected herself and was optimistic she'd be able to act like a functioning witch and speak in a normal tone from now on. Even if she was a total mess on the inside, having broken the ice with a little banter made her feel more confident in her abilities to fake it until she made it.

"So, who are we going to interrogate first?" she asked.

He threw her a side glance as if he was ready to call bullshit at her nonchalant tone, but soon his eyes flickered back to the road and he answered her. "I thought the angry soccer mom would be our best bet."

Mila nodded in agreement. "Oh, that's going to be so much fun."

Riley's mouth tilted up at the corners, and Mila did her best not to think how wickedly good that same mouth had felt on hers as he devoured her. Or about the trail of fire those same lips had left on her jaw and neck and collarbone as he'd kissed his way down her body.

And, once again, she was failing miserably...

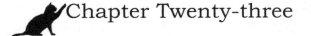

Chapter Twenty-three

Take a Chill Pill

RILEY

The gated community where Mrs. Princeton and her family lived was one of the most exclusive residential neighborhoods in Salem. Made entirely of lush mansions with perfectly landscaped front yards and an array of luxury cars parked in the driveways that could rival a sheik.

Riley flashed his badge to the security guard manning the entrance, eager to get out of the car and put a healthy distance between himself and Mila Bennet. The few scrawny inches currently separating them in the car would not cut it.

This morning, she'd chosen to torture him with a fluffy, purple-and-black striped sweater wool dress that made her look totally huggable. He wanted to bury his face in that dress. Pull it over her head and uncover the marvels underneath.

The need was so strong he had to clutch the wheel harder to stop himself from doing something incredibly stupid.

In the meantime, the security guard had taken one look at Riley's badge and waved them past the gate. At its very foundation, The Department of Magical Justice was enchanted to confound humans. The protective thrall was needed for its agent to conduct investigations in the human world without kicking up a fuss or causing raised eyebrows among humans. It was a necessary protective charm essential to guarantee seamless cooperation and coexistence between the magical law enforcement agencies and the regular human ones.

Riley took his badge back, rolled up the window, and drove on until they reached the cul-de-sac at the end of the community.

Mrs. Princeton's house was easily the most opulent in the entire neighborhood, surely the most extravagantly decorated for Christmas, with a real-life-sized illuminated sleigh in the front yard, pulled by a full battery of six reindeer. Fairy lights dotted the entire surface of the house's external walls.

The lights were glittering in a rainbow of colors even now that it was broad daylight.

Riley got out of the car and waited for

Mila—not getting the door for her. If she didn't want him to open doors for her, she was entitled to renounce the gallantry.

As they walked up the driveway of the flashy mansion, Mila stared at the extravagant décor of the house, wide-eyed and open-mouthed. "How much do you think their electricity bill comes to?"

Riley suppressed a smile. "I don't know, but I'm pretty sure they're at least five percent responsible for global warming."

Mila looked up at him, her eyes twinkling with amusement from under her long lashes. Riley had to shove his hands into his pocket not to reach over and tuck a loose curl of that impossibly long, impossibly silky hair behind her ear.

It would be ages, possibly forever, before he forgot how her hair had felt tangled in his fingers as they kissed.

Mila must've sensed his thoughts had shifted away from electrical fixtures and degenerated into something entirely different because she cleared her throat and looked away from him.

And he was acting like a troll again.

Riley quickened his stride and reached the front door two steps ahead of Mila, ringing the bell.

Maybe discussing the attempted murder of Mrs. Blackwell with a suspect would help him take a chill pill.

 # Chapter Twenty-four

That Was Mean

MILA

Mila stepped on the porch behind Riley, marveling at the fact that the snow under her feet wasn't melting away and running down the front steps in steaming rivulets. She was boiling inside her coat, and she was sure some of the heat must be transferring to the surrounding environment. At the current rate of heated gazes she and Riley were sharing, Mila was sure they'd be one-hundred percent responsible for global warming.

But jumping gargoyles, if he didn't stop looking at her like he had just now on the driveway—as if he wanted to get rid of all of their clothes and explore every inch of her body with his mouth—she might combust right there on the porch.

Thankfully, it didn't take long for Mrs. Princeton to come to the door, even if she appeared slightly out of breath as she threw the door ajar.

She was wearing only a pastel winter robe and pale pink slipper boots. Her state of agitation visibly worsened as she took in the tall, unforgiving form of Riley presently standing on her doorstep with his bad-cop mask on.

A reaction Mila could sympathize with all too well.

Mrs. Princeton quickly straightened the lapels of her robe and flattened her blonde hair. "Morning, Detective," she said.

The security guard at the gate must've alerted her of their arrival.

"Morning, Mrs. Princeton. I'm Detective King from Salem PD." Riley flashed her his badge, and as it happened with all humans coming in contact with magical law enforcement, her eyes glazed over slightly—the incantation protecting the secrecy of the wizarding world working its magic. "And this is my associate, Detective Bennet."

Not exactly factual, but Mila liked the ring her fake new title had.

"Good morning," she greeted Mrs. Princeton in what she hoped sounded like a bad-cop voice.

Only Riley stared down at her with a puzzled look, so maybe she'd only greeted the suspect in a *ridiculous* voice.

Better let the expert conduct the interview, then.

"We would like to talk to you about the

happenings of last night at Swift River Elementary, if you could spare a minute."

"Sure. Please, Detectives, come on in." She opened the door wider for them to enter.

The giant house seemed to be empty except for her and a mean-looking white cat lounging on the couch.

As if Mrs. Princeton had read Mila's mind, she said, "My husband already went back to work." She let out a high-pitched giggle. "Apparently a one-day holiday was already a stretch for him, and my kids are upstairs, doing who knows what? Can I offer you anything to drink? Tea, coffee?"

Riley politely declined, and Mila followed his lead.

They sat in the living room, and Mila took pains to give a wide berth to the white cat. Animals, contrary to humans, were far the wiser about the existence of magic and were better equipped to sense the presence of a witch or a wizard.

"What can I help you with, Detectives?" Mrs. Princeton asked from her perch on the couch opposite them.

"You were at your daughter's Christmas recital last night, Mrs. Princeton, correct?"

The woman's nose twisted in a faintly

disgusted expression. "I was, even if only briefly."

"You mean you didn't stay until the end?"

"No, why would I?"

Riley frowned. "Your daughter was in the play, wasn't she?"

Mrs. Princeton winced. "She only had a minor part in the first act, and Tory's performance was the only one I cared about. Once I saw her, I left."

"You left alone, though. Your husband stayed behind?"

"Well, someone had to bring Tory home afterward."

"Did you and your husband go to the school in separate vehicles?"

"No, same car."

"How did you get home, then?"

"I called an Uber. Why?"

"Did you keep a receipt for the ride?"

"Yeah, sure, on my phone." Mrs. Princeton made to stand up, then plonked back down on the couch, eying us warily. "Why are you asking me all these questions?"

"Are you aware of what happened to Mrs. Blackwell at the end of the show?"

"You mean that old hag half chocking to death on a cupcake? Can't say I'm sorry."

Riley's face remained impassible, even if Mila could sense distaste wash over him in waves. Still, seeing him in his element was hot, *so frogging hot*. All that restrained power contained in such a handsome package threatened to make her whimper just for having to witness it.

Voice colder than the icicles dangling from the gutters outside, Riley said, "Mrs. Blackwell was actually poisoned and is currently struggling for her life at Mass General Brigham Hospital."

Mrs. Princeton seemed genuinely taken aback. "Oh, I'm sorry to hear." Then her eyes widened. "Wait, you don't think *I* had anything to do with it?"

"Several eye witnesses reported you being involved in a heated argument with Mrs. Blackwell over your daughter not playing the principal role in the recital."

"Well, sure. That woman couldn't recognize talent if it stared her right in the face. She kept insisting that my daughter wasn't good enough for the lead role, even though she's clearly the most talented child in that class. But that doesn't mean I tried to kill her."

"Did anyone see you get back home, Mrs. Princeton?"

The soccer mom's voice was becoming shriller by the minute. "The Uber driver and the night guard outside. They keep a log of everyone who comes and goes."

"And after that?" Riley insisted. "You spent the rest of the night home alone?"

"Yes."

"Can anyone confirm it?"

Genuine panic crossed Mrs. Princeton's face for the first time. "Well, no. I don't know what time Roger and Tory came back, but I was already sleeping."

"What about your son?" I ask. "Where was he?"

"Out with friends."

"So you have no confirmed alibi," Riley concluded.

Mila had to suppress a smirk. She was sure he was laying it on thick only because he disliked Mrs. Princeton. And how to blame him?

Abruptly, he stood up. "Very well, Mrs. Princeton. We'll get in touch if we have more questions."

Mila got up as well.

"Wait." Mrs. Princeton stood up as well and followed them to the door. "Are you actually saying that I'm a suspect?" The last word came out indignant.

With a stony face, Riley said, "Salem PD investigations are confidential, but I wouldn't leave the country if I were you."

Mrs. Princeton visibly gulped. "All right, Detective."

Riley nodded severely and proceeded down the driveway without another word. Mila caught up with him about halfway down and bumped shoulders with him. "That parting salvo was mean. I bet you scared her half to death."

"That woman is obnoxious. A little fear will do her good."

"But you don't think she did it, right?"

"We have to verify her story with the security guard up front. But even if her account checks out, she could've still come home and then gone back out to the school..."

They stopped before the car.

"I don't know," Mila reasoned. "The more I think about it, the less likely it seems Mrs. Princeton did it."

"How come?" Riley frowned in that adorable, impossibly sexy way of his.

Mila ignored her mounting lust, and answered him, "From what we know, the killer only poisoned one cupcake, otherwise more people would've fallen ill. So, he or she must've poisoned the cupcake and then delivered it straight to Mrs. Blackwell to make sure their intended victim ate it. I don't see Mrs. Princeton walking back into a party where everyone thought she'd already stormed out, then taking a poisoned cupcake to the woman she'd just had an all-out verbal brawl with."

"Maybe she presented it as a peace offering."

"Maybe, but I still don't see it. I'll ask my sister and my parents if they saw Mrs. Princeton anywhere in that gym. We could ask the same question also to the other witches present, check the security footage of the school entrance. But it's still more likely that Mrs. Blackwell accepted the cupcake from someone she knew and trusted."

Riley studied her for a second. "Which brings us on to our next suspect, the grandson."

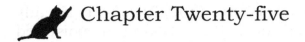 Chapter Twenty-five

The Hidden Dangers of Coffee Shops

RILEY

They were back in his car. Back to being stuck into a too-compact space together. Riley had better solve this case fast, or he'd lose his sanity.

The silence between them stretched, fast-approaching awkward.

Riley was frantically searching his brain for something harmless to say, when Mila beat him to it.

"I get it why we can't accept refreshments from suspects," she mused.

Riley turned to her with a raised eyebrow. "And why is that?"

Mila frowned adorably. "It wouldn't be professional."

"That's not why I refused the offer. Coffee is hardly a bribe."

"Why'd you refuse, then?"

"I just wanted to be rid of that woman's company as fast as possible."

"Oh, okay."

"Why, you wanted to accept?"

"Maybe, I mean, the Potentilla Latte

was great, but would you think me greedy if I asked to stop for another cup of coffee on the way?"

Would you think me greedy if I asked to kiss you now until the end of eternity? Riley thought and was never more glad for the beanie shielding Mila from all his improprieties. "Regular shop or witchy one?"

The good thing about living in a town like Salem for a wizard was that humans didn't as much as raise an eyebrow if a coffee shop owner wrote on his blackboard a selection of wizarding drinks including dragonfire ale, unicorn's milk, blackberry grog, starlight cider, batwing coffee, or eyes of newt bubble tea.

Humans who ordered one of these specials would get served regular spiced hot beverages, while the wizards and witches in town would get the real thing.

"Witchy," Mila said. "I could do with the extra kick."

Couldn't they all?

***

The request for a coffee break had seemed innocuous enough when Riley had agreed to it. But he was fast learning that danger lay also in the most unsuspected places when Mila Bennet was involved.

Take an action as simple as drinking a froggucino. It was completely innocent in theory. But not when the foamy drink left a white mustache over Mila's upper lip that begged to be licked off.

Before he knew what he was doing, Riley wiped it clean with his thumb, and then, not content, he sucked his finger clean.

And that wasn't even the worst part.

The worst part was how Mila's eyes trailed the gesture to his mouth and how, immediately after, her gaze snapped up to meet his. He could drown in that stare, drown in a pool of molten lava, given the heat he could read in her green irises.

Apparently, getting coffee with Mila Bennet was a big no-no. Like sitting in a car with her. Or having dinner together. No action, no matter how mundane, was safe around her.

"Sorry," Riley apologized because he couldn't just go and act like that and then pretend it hadn't happened. "I don't know why I did it."

Mila's features hardened with guilt. "We both know it's the potion. I'm so sorry I've cursed you into being attracted to me, Riley."

The only curse was not being able to *act* on that attraction. Riley hated the guilt on Mila's face with an intensity that churned in his chest and replaced his heart with a swirling, raging black hole of regret. But letting her experience this momentary guilt was the lesser evil compared to the suffering and devastation the alternative would bring.

Still, he could try to make her feel more at ease.

"Hey, at least I've been bewitched by a beautiful enchantress with spectacular green eyes and long mermaid hair."

She just gaped at him.

"You could've been an old hag."

Now she scowled, working hard to contain the smile that was tugging at her lips. "With that love potion, you would've liked me even if I'd been an old hag."

Riley shrugged. "I seriously doubt it."

"Then you're seriously wrong."

"I'm rarely wrong."

"You were wrong when you arrested me and my sister."

"Technically, I wasn't. You'd still violated the law, and I was just following procedure."

"Then procedure sucks."

"Careful, Miss Bennet, that sounded a lot like insubordination."

She flipped him the bird. "And how's this for insubordination?"

Riley threw his head back and laughed.

Mila pouted in response. "I'm so going to turn you into a toad."

Riley gently grabbed her arm and leaned in to whisper in her ear. "Maybe we should stop discussing love potions and turning anyone into toads in a coffee shop full of tourists."

Getting so close to her was clearly another mistake, as the scent of that maddeningly good coconut shampoo invaded his nostrils. On top of that, he could now perceive the slight tremor his whispering in her ear had sent down her body.

Riley felt his own body respond with a surge of desire, and he quickly straightened up, hoping to hide his reaction.

Easier said than done when the air between them had thickened, and become charged with an electricity that neither of them could escape.

Mila's cheeks flushed a soft pink, and she bit her lip, clearly experiencing the same discomfort.

Riley stared at her mouth for a too-long instant, then forced his gaze away.

Get a grip, man, he chided himself.

But he couldn't, not while she was so close. The only effective solution would be *not* to be in Mila Bennet's proximity, and that could happen only when they solved the case.

On that note, Riley proceeded to the coffee shop exit and held the door open for Mila. "Break over, Bennet. We have a loose wannabe murderer to catch."

Mila rolled her eyes but couldn't suppress the smile that crept onto her face. She walked out, flipping her hair back. "Lead the way, Detective."

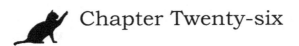 # Chapter Twenty-six

Aerials

MILA

They were stuck in his car, again. Only this time it looked like it was going to be ten thousand times worse because they'd be here a while.

They'd gone to Trent Blackwell's house, but Mrs. Blackwell's grandson wasn't home, and now Mila and Riley were waiting for him, out parked on his street.

The car engine was turned off and so was the heating, but Riley had wrapped that warm air blanket around them to avoid them turning into popsicles.

The air blanket was cozy, perhaps *too* cozy. Mila felt it brush against her cheeks like a balmy caress. She felt it also at the back of her neck, tangling in her hair, massaging her scalp. She couldn't shake the sensation that the air felt like deft fingers—Riley's fingers—moving over her body, fondling her with gentle strokes.

But Mila couldn't be sure. She couldn't know if Riley was even aware he was doing it or if his air was simply misbehaving. What she knew for sure was that if the treatment continued—potion or no potion, right or wrong—she'd straddle Riley and kiss him until there'd be no more air left to breathe in this hexing car.

"Where do you think he's gone?" Mila asked to distract herself.

Riley shrugged. "He could be everywhere, out with friends, to see another family member, with his girlfriend, or visiting the hospital even."

Yeah, that didn't help. Neither did the warm air now caressing her calves. Mila shifted in her seat, hoping Riley wouldn't notice the flush that was creeping up her neck.

She cleared her throat. "Is there some background check we can do on him while we wait?"

Riley's gaze flickered over to her, its intensity overwhelming. "What do you mean?"

"I don't know. Check with your people at the hospital if he even went there to visit, and what their impression of him was?"

"You mean loving grandson worried sick for his gran or gold digger eager for the old fart to bite the dust?"

Mila chuckled, but the smile died on

her lips as the warm air fingers moved up to the back of her knees, stroking the crease that joined her lower and upper legs. All Mila could do was nod in response, suppressing a whimper.

Seemingly unaware of her predicament, Riley nodded. "I can call Sarah Michelle. It's her shift at the hospital."

That's when the air moved up her thighs, and Mila couldn't take it any longer. "Can you please tell your air to stop?"

Riley turned to her with a puzzled look on his face. "What?"

The air had now reached her inner thighs and Mila was this close to coming undone right there, right now in Riley's car. "Your air is..." Mila bit her lower lip, trying to find the right words, but there was no easy way to put it. "Sort of *fondling me.* Can you make it stop?"

Riley froze, and so did the car.

The warmth, the fingers made of breeze and magic, were both gone in an instant. Mila shivered in the sudden cold, while Riley simply shook his head and got out of the car, saying, "I'll call Detective Callidora. You use your own warming spell."

Then he slammed the car door shut

and was out on the curb, one hand shoving through his hair under the beanie while he pinched in the number on his phone with the other.

Mila sagged back on the seat. Oh, hell, she only had to make it to tomorrow night. Then Judge Templeton would assign her to a different community service, and this nightmare of uncontrollable want that was pulling at every inch of her skin from the inside would be gone.

Outside the car, Riley had ended the call, but it looked like he had no intention of coming back in. So Mila got out.

"Found out anything?" she asked casually.

Riley stared at her for a long moment, his eyes on her almost harder to bear than his aerial hands. Then he nodded. "Apparently, Trent is a devoted grandson and has been Mrs. Blackwell's most assiduous visitor." He shoved that hand through his hair again, scratching himself under the beanie, and looked away from her as he kept talking. "My agents report that he's been spending hours at Mrs. Blackwell's bedside, reading a story to her."

"Genuine love, or an act to cover his tracks?"

Riley shrugged. "I don't know. But Sarah Michelle told me he just left a few minutes ago, saying he was headed home. So, we can expect him back any minute now."

And just as well. If Riley and Mila had to spend another prolonged period alone together, she was afraid they'd explode from all the tension that had been boiling up non-stop for two days now.

Only one more day to go, Mila repeated to herself. *You can do it.*

Chapter Twenty-seven

You Got Plenty of Game

RILEY

Riley was still too shamefaced to meet Mila's gaze. So while they waited for Trent Blackwell to get the hex back home, he paced the curb and put as much distance between himself and the witch as he could without being too obvious or rude.

In the car, while they'd been waiting for Mrs. Blackwell's grandson, he had been imagining touching Mila. Every inch of her body. He'd started at her scalp, walking his way down her arms to the sides of her legs until he'd reached her ankles to then reverse his trail in the opposite direction, moving up her thighs. And if Mila had felt every single one of those touches... Riley suppressed a groan. Well, let's just say she'd stopped him barely in time before he did something really, *really* inappropriate.

As they waited, Riley's mind kept wandering back to that moment in the car. He didn't know how much longer he could hold out. He found himself almost hoping Trent Blackwell was a homicidal maniac so he could close the case and get back to his simple, Mila-Bennet-free life.

Finally, a dark figure huddled in a long winter coat strutted up Trent Blackwell's driveway—that must've been him.

Riley waved at Mila, and they followed the man to his house.

Ten minutes later, as they sat in Trent Blackwell's living room, both nursing a much-needed cup of chamomile infusion, it was clear their second suspect was no murdering scumbag. He was practically a saint.

"I understand why you're here, Detectives," he said, plunging the chamomile bag in and out of the hot water in his cup. "Someone told you I'm a greedy moneygrubber who spends time with his grandmother only to make sure I'll inherit her fortune one day."

Riley waited for him to go on. Asking the grandson to clarify that he was not, in fact, a moneygrubbing leech felt like overkill.

"But that's not the relationship I have with Nan at all. We've always been close, even before I grasped the concept of rich and poor."

"You mean when you were a child?" Mila asked. She seemed prone to believe the sanctitude act, which, in all fairness, seemed genuine.

Trent Blackwell shrugged. "She basically raised me. My grandfather was the rich one. He died young, and Nan never remarried. So, she came into her inheritance still relatively young, but she never passed any of it on to my father, wanting him to make his own path in life. And that's exactly what he did"—Trent stared out the window with a regretful expression—"his career has always been his priority. Nan went into teaching because, well, she liked drama and she liked the relaxed hours a part-time job as a drama teacher afforded her, giving her plenty of time to spend with her only grandkid." He pointed a thumb at himself. "My parents never complained. They liked the free babysitting and added freedom, so in the end, everyone got what they wanted."

Mila spoke next. "Did your grandmother pass any money on to you, or does she still have full control of her fortune?"

"Good intuition, Detective Bennet."

The grandson flashed Mila a grin, and Riley bristled. Trent Blackwell would stop looking at Mila with such unadulterated appreciation if he knew what was good for him.

"Yes," the grandson confirmed. "We don't like to advertise it, so not many people outside the family know about it, but she's been looser with me. She bought me this house"—he gestured at the surrounding walls—"And gave me enough financial independence for me to choose a job I love without worrying about money too much."

Riley was almost afraid to ask. "And what is it you do, Mr. Blackwell?"

"I'm a psychologist. I work with special needs people, children in school in particular." A saint indeed, Riley thought. "The goal is mainly to avoid having students with disabilities being marginalized from the rest of the student population and reinforce the concept with educators that most special need students can achieve the same academic standards as their nondisabled peers. That's why I was at the recital. One of my students was in the play. I wasn't there to kiss Nan's ass or to kill her to put my hands on the money she's already given me."

Oh, at least Mr. Perfect was capable of a little swearing, otherwise Riley was ready to conjure a bona fide halo and place it upon his head.

"Any idea who would wish your

grandmother harm, Mr. Blackwell?" Mila asked the next logical question.

"She had recently ended a relationship with one of her Buraco mates, and from what she'd told me, the gentleman hadn't taken the news too well. But Jacob Sheridan seemed genuinely in love with her, and I never pegged him down as a violent man."

Riley refrained from saying that poison was the exact opposite of violence. "Did you know if your grandmother had started seeing anyone else?"

"I'm pretty sure she had, and that she was keeping the relationship secret to spare Jacob's feelings."

Out of the corner of his eye, Riley caught Mila making a funny face and suppressing a grin.

What in the hex had she to laugh about?

Piqued by curiosity, Riley shifted the beanie off his head and sent her a mental prod. *"Why are you smirking?"*

Mila's eyes widened, and she stared at him in surprise. Then she lifted her cup to her lips to hide her widening smirk and sent him a telepathic reply, *"Oh, nothing, I just find it ironic that Mrs. Blackwell is closer to seventy than sixty and she's still got more game at her age than I do a twenty-nine."*

"You got plenty of game, Bennet."

She crossed her eyes. *"Oh, please, we both know that unless I curse unsuspecting inquisitors, I have exactly zero game."*

That's when Trent Blackwell interrupted their mental sparring. "Is there something else you wanted to ask me, Detectives?"

Riley shot a furtive look at Mila and silently asked, *"Do you believe him?"*

She nodded and replied equally silently, *"I do."*

Riley pushed the beanie back onto his head and stood up. "No, thank you, Mr. Blackwell. That'd be all for today. Thanks again for your availability, and if you can think of anything else, please don't hesitate to call us. I hope to report progress on the case soon."

"I'm the grateful one, Detective King, for the opportunity to clear my name. I hope you find the actual attempted killer soon."

Riley walked out of Trent Blackwell's house feeling despondent. This had been another giant hole in the water, and they weren't any closer to solving the case.

But at least now it was too late to go interrogate Mrs. Blackwell's former lover, which meant he could drive Mila Bennet home and then go back to his place to sulk in misery all night, lay awake tormented by dreams of being with her, and then get up in the morning to go pick her up and start that circus all over again.

Chapter Twenty-eight

Brooders and Broomsticks

MILA

The next morning Mila had contrasting feelings about seeing Riley. On the one hand, she was relieved today would be the last day she'd be forced to spend with him. On the other, she was devastated for the exact reason.

Especially when she went to open her door and found him on her porch as spine-tinglingly handsome as ever in his dark clothes and equally unsettling black eyes. Only this time, he was also holding her broomstick in his hands.

For a moment, Mila forgot her woes and grabbed the broom from his outstretched arms, holding it like a dance partner and twirling it around with her along the porch.

Then she laid the broomstick against the outer wall of her house and instinctively hugged Riley. "Thanks for bringing Clarabella back."

He remained rigid in her arms at first, but she gave him a couple of extra seconds until he engulfed her completely in his warmth. His hands wrapped around her waist and settled on the small of her back.

"You named your broom Clarabella?" he whispered, his lips brushing the top of her head.

She pulled back just enough to look up at him. "Why? You keep a nameless broom? That seems awfully mean."

He smirked down at her. "Brooms are not sentient."

"Says who? Clarabella and I had many a conversation while up in the starry sky."

Mila was well aware she should let go of him. Instead, she did just the opposite. She dropped her head back in the nook of his shoulder and squeezed harder. After all, today was the last day she had with him. She might as well enjoy it and suffer through it while it lasted. "But thank you for bringing her back."

He dropped his chin on top of her head and started stroking her hair in a regular rhythm. "The weather has cleared, and I thought you might miss flying."

Mila kept her face hidden in his chest as a million thoughts assaulted her. Had Riley somehow sensed that he wouldn't be driving her around after today, that this was their last day together? He was the son of the most potent seer on the east coast, after all. Maybe some of his mother's power had rubbed off on him.

Whatever the reason he had to bring the broomstick back today, Mila was all the more grateful. It'd make reaching the DMJ for her appointment with Judge Templeton later today much simpler, especially since she was wearing pants— much more appropriate clothes to fly. But it also made letting go of Riley that much harder.

"Hey," he said now above her head, his voice laced with gentleness and perhaps a hint of regret? "I thought you were supposed to turn me into a toad, not that I would turn you into a koala bear."

Mila couldn't help but laugh, the sound bubbling up from her chest and spilling out into the open air. "Don't you like koala bears, Riley?" she asked with a smile, feeling his hands stilling in her hair as she pronounced his name.

"I love koala bears." The stroking resumed. "But unfortunately, we still have an attempted murder to solve."

Using every last ounce of her willpower, Mila let him go and pulled back.

"I believe we do," Mila said, trying to sound as focused as possible. "Let's go grill our last potential suspect."

Riley draped an arm over her shoulder, and they walked down her driveway side by side, like Mila imagined a couple in love would do. If only their love was real and not a byproduct of her reckless potion-making.

As they drove toward Mr. Sheridan's house, Mila spent the entire journey stealing glances at Riley. At his chiseled features, sharp jawline, and pillow lips she'd no longer see, no longer kiss, trying to memorize every square inch of his face.

She tried to keep the sadness at bay, but a raging panic was overpowering every sense of relief she'd initially had at the thought that their brief, unsettling acquaintance would soon be over.

Too soon and not nearly soon enough, they were pulling up in front of Jacob Sheridan's house. He lived in an apartment complex made of three-story buildings with beige wooden siding and small brown balconies.

Mr. Sheridan was in unit 2B and came to open the door soon after Riley's first knock.

"Ah, yeah." He didn't seem surprised at finding two law enforcement agents on his doorstep. In fact, the next words out of his mouth were "I was wondering when you'd show up. Took you long enough."

Was he confessing? Or was he just being flippant?

Mila studied Mr. Sheridan, taking in his slicked-back white hair and shiny suit. She couldn't get a read on him, but something about his demeanor made her uneasy.

Riley stepped forward, his badge held up in front of him.

"Mr. Sheridan, we'd like to ask you a few questions regarding the attempted murder of your former partner, Mrs. Blackwell," Riley said, his voice calm but assertive.

The man nodded and opened the door wider. "Come on in, then."

He was the first of their persons of interest not to offer them any refreshment. And just as well. Similarly to Riley with their first suspect, Mrs. Princeton, Mila couldn't wait to get this interrogation over with. Mr. Sheridan was a truly unpleasant man who gave her strong, icky vibes.

But was he a killer or just an insufferable, rude, old grump?

"Mr. Sheridan—" Riley started as soon as they were seated in his living room.

But the man interrupted him with a raised hand. "I know what you're about to ask, but I didn't do it. I love Josephine. I want her back. I don't want her dead."

"Mr. Sheridan, were you aware that Mrs. Blackwell is in another relationship at the moment?"

The man jumped up on his couch. "Why? You know who it's with?" But before Riley could respond, the man continued. "No need. I'm pretty sure I already know it's that MacNeil backstabber."

The name sounded familiar to Mila, and she did a quick search of the notes on her phone. "You mean George Harrison MacNeil?"

"Yeah, just the ruffian."

Riley gave her a quiet nod, letting her take the lead. "He's in your Buraco club, right?"

"Unfortunately."

Mila kept scrolling her notes. "But aren't he and Cherry Knox in a relationship? We saw them at the hospital together the other day visiting Mrs. Blackwell."

Mr. Sheridan puffed out his cheeks. "Oh, I bet the old hag would love to get her spiky claws into MacNeil, but he only ever had eyes for my Josephine. I'm pretty sure he's the one who stole her away." The note of visceral pain in the man's voice sounded genuine.

Mila still didn't like him very much, but she was also starting to believe he had had nothing to do with the poisoning.

"Are you sure nothing is going on between Mrs. Knox and Mr. MacNeil?"

Mr. Sheridan gave her an empty stare, shaking his head. "At this point, I'm not sure of anything."

Riley and Mila thanked the old man and took their leave, stopping to regroup outside his building.

"I don't think he did it," Mila said.

"Neither do I," Riley agreed.

"So, what's our next move?"

"I think we need to pay Mr. MacNeil a visit, see if he truly is Mrs. Blackwell's new boyfriend, and if that leads to something else."

***

Only when they got to Mr. MacNeil's house, he wasn't home. They waited him out, sharing a sandwich in Riley's car, no naughty heating provided. But when the evening started to fall and Mr. MacNeil still hadn't shown up, Mila had to ask Riley to bring her back home.

"Sorry," she apologized. "But I have an appointment, and I can't be late."

Riley seemed to struggle for a second not to ask with whom or what the appointment was about, but in the end, he simply nodded and drove her home in silence.

When he stopped in front of her house, he had no idea how momentous the goodbyes were. That this would be their final act.

He simply turned to her, not even killing the car engine, and said, "Same time tomorrow, Bennet?"

She just nodded because words escaped her. And she was afraid that even if she managed to talk, she'd just implode and start all-out bawling, which wouldn't be ideal if she wanted to keep her plan to free Riley of her forced proximity on the down-low.

Before she could change her mind altogether and grab his beautiful face to kiss him and never again let go, Mila exited the car and ran up her driveway.

Maybe it was best that he didn't know what was happening. Best that he didn't get to ask questions or look sad or even have a say in her decision.

Mila slammed into her front door, using magic instead of her keys to fling it open, and got inside, away from him, away from her stupid feelings.

Gargoyles, her high school potion teacher really must've been the worst judge of academic talent for almost failing her in his class. If the heart-wrenching intensity of her pulse now was any indication of her abilities, she'd turned out to be an excellent potion maker.

Chapter Twenty-nine

Buckle Up

MILA

Mila was exceedingly nervous as she waited outside Judge Templeton's office. True, the judge's office was in an entirely separate wing of the DMJ building with respect to the police station. But that didn't stop Mila from worrying she'd run into Riley. This was his turf, after all.

Even if he had most probably gone home after dropping her off, one could never know. He seemed a bit of a workaholic.

Finally, after long, interminable minutes in the waiting room, a clerk called her name and showed her inside the judge's office.

It was a large room with an impressive mahogany desk at the center, covered in scattered papers and writing implements of different sorts, a contrast to the otherwise tidy room lined with filing cabinets and neatly organized bookshelves. The office smelled like a combination of expensive leather and old parchment, with a hint of sandalwood.

Judge Templeton sat behind the desk, her head bent over a thick file. As Mila entered, the judge looked up, her sharp eyes analyzing Mila from head to toe before she motioned for her to take a seat in one of the two chairs in front of the desk.

"Ah, Miss Bennet." Judge Templeton reclined in her leather chair, lacing her fingers over her lap. "I admit I was surprised to find you in my appointment book today. What can I do for you?"

Still rather nervous, Mila thought it best not to circle around the issue. Judge Templeton seemed like a direct witch, with no patience for niceties. "Hello, Your Honor. I've come to ask to be assigned to a different community service for my sentence."

Judge Templeton tilted her head and let the request hang in the suddenly suffocating silence of the room for a while. "Investigative work doesn't suit you?"

"No, I like the work. I enjoy it a lot," Mila said truthfully. The last few days had reminded her why she'd gotten her private investigator license. "It's not the job. It's my partner."

Judge Templeton's eyebrow disappeared under her bangs. "Chief

King isn't acting like a gentleman?"

"No, no, of course, he is." Mila pushed her hands forward in his defense. "He's been nothing other than a gentleman, Your Honor, truly." Well, except maybe for that time he'd pressed her against the wall and kissed the hex out of her. Or when he'd then carried her to his bedroom and pressed her even harder into the mattress underneath him. Or that time when his air spells had gotten a little handsy. Mila blushed and forced her brain to stay focused on the matter at hand. After all, none of those reactions on Riley's part had been voluntary. "Riley has been a brilliant partner, really," Mila insisted.

"Riley?" Judge Templeton seemed taken aback at her use of his first name, but she moved on. "Then what's the matter?"

"I might've accidentally cursed him?"

"Miss Bennet." The judge gave up all appearances of coolness and dropped her elbows on her desk, taking her head in her hands while massaging her temples with her fingers. "I met you not two days ago, after you'd involuntarily cursed half the town's elementary school with an illegal love elixir. As penance, I've sentenced you to help Salem MPD solve the attempted murder your potion has coincidentally thwarted, and you mean to tell me that, in the two days since I've last seen you, instead of reflecting on your mistakes, you've also managed to accidentally curse our Chief Inquisitor?"

Well, when she put it like that, Mila's character came out a little worse for wear. But Mila had her response at the ready. "Judge Templeton, believe me, in the last two days, I've done nothing more than reflect on my poor life's choices. But Inquisitor King's curse is still part of the original mistake."

Judge Templeton dropped one hand and kept massaging her forehead with the other. "How do you mean?"

"See, the potion I brewed was supposed to make me fall in love with the first man I saw, and for that love to be reciprocated. I made the cupcakes, ate one, and then I went to take a bath and fell asleep in the tub..."

Judge Templeton made a twirling gesture with her fingers as if to say, *I already know all of that. Please move along,* so Mila came to the conclusion, "And, well, when I woke up, Riley was arresting me. He was the first man I saw, you see, which of course triggered the effects of the potion, and so... umm...

working with him these past few days...
err... things have gotten a little... mmm...
complicated. Riley is attracted to me, and
he can't help it because I've cursed him
into it, and I feel the same, *obviously*, but
still only because of the potion... so, err,
it'd be better if we were no longer bound
to work together. Mostly for Riley's sake.
He didn't ask for this, but we can both
agree I had it coming..."

The judge was now sitting straight in
her chair. "Miss Bennet, how did this
attraction between you and Chief King
manifest, if I may ask?"

Mila thought of all the wall pressing
and mattress pressing, of the handsy air,
and stolen glances, and Riley wiping
froggucino foam off her upper lip and
then licking his thumb, and blushed. "Is
it really relevant?"

"No." Judge Templeton shook her
head. "As a matter of fact, it isn't. I
assume you've shared this theory of
yours with Chief King?"

Mila nodded.

"And out of curiosity, how did he
respond?"

"Why do you need to know?"

"Just humor me, please, Miss
Bennet."

Mila wrung her fingers, feeling all the

more mortified. "He agreed we shouldn't act on a potion-induced attraction and should keep things professional until we could solve the case and move on with our lives."

"I see," the judge said, once again reclining in her chair. "I probably shouldn't share this with you, Miss Bennet, but you're about the same age as my daughter and sometimes you remind me of her so much. Therefore, I'm going to go out on a limb for you and let you in on a little secret."

Mila waited with a beating heart, ready to discover the secret meaning of life.

"All magical law enforcement officers," Judge Templeton continued, "are warded against all kinds of wayward spells and courses, even black magic. Their special protective gear shields them from about anything short of Dragonfire. It'd take a truly powerful witch or wizard with a lot of intent to breach through that kind of safeguard. And I don't mean to question your potion-making skills, but I seriously doubt that your incantation affected Chief King in any sort of way."

"But, but... he didn't tell me any of this. Why?"

Judge Templeton sighed. "I might not be the person you want to ask that question to."

Mila was still a little stunned. "I'm sorry, Your Honor, but my potion must've still worked at least on me because then how would you explain my side of the *thing*?"

The judge gave her a long stare. "Miss Bennet, do I really have to spell it out for you? You're young, and Chief King, in case you haven't noticed, is a really attractive wiz—"

"No, that's not it," Mila protested, not even caring that she was interrupting a judge. "I could feel the magic between us, I swear. The potion must've worked at least on me, or his gear must've malfunctioned and let the magic through."

"That's highly improbable."

"But not impossible, right?"

Judge Templeton seemed to be losing her patience fast now. Any goodwill Mila might've had with her was quickly evaporating. The judge started rummaging through the various court files on her desk until she presumably found the one she was looking for and started sorting through the pages with curt, annoyed flips until she clicked her tongue and stared down at Mila with an air of victory. "Miss Bennet, how well did you pay attention in your defensive magic classes in school?"

Mila had never been to the top of her class, but also not at the bottom. Still, right now, she felt like she was being interrogated for a test she hadn't prepared for. "I did okay, I guess."

"All right, it says here that on the night of your arrest, you were accidentally stunned. Is that correct?"

"Yes."

"And that happened before you saw Chief King."

Mila nodded again.

"Then as you surely can remember from your studies, the primary effect of being stunned is to have one's magic temporarily tempered, but the shock doesn't stop just at the power of the witch or wizard who has been hit, it also wipes all other enchantments or curses. In fact, stunning is one of the most used techniques in counter magimedicine."

Mila pressed the heels of her palms over her eyes and shook her head. "That is not possible. There must be another explanation."

"Miss Bennet, why are you so hellbent on denying a simple attraction between a witch and a wizard? I know Chief King must not seem like the most approachable—"

"Because we share a mental bond," Mila shouted, lowering her hands from her face and confessing the secret she hadn't dared tell anyone, except for her familiar. That was enough to finally shock the judge into silence. "And I know witches can't share mental bonds unless they're related. So, unless you're about to tell me that Riley is my secret brother, there must be some other explanation. Magic is connecting us somehow, and the only logical explanation is that it must be because of the love potion. My stunning wasn't thorough, or Riley's gear somehow failed to protect him, but it must be something."

After her tirade, Judge Templeton sat so still for so long that Mila wondered if she wasn't, in fact, a gargoyle who had momentarily turned to stone.

Then the judge made Mila jolt in her chair as she abruptly stood up to scan the magical manuals on her bookshelves. She scanned the spines of the old tomes until she settled on the smaller, most-ancient-looking one.

She brought the book back to her desk and, flipping to the section that presumably interested her, Judge Templeton started reading.

Mila tried to elongate her neck and peek at the text, but the writing was too thin for her to decipher. What wasn't hard to interpret was the increasingly more prominent look of consternation on the judge's face.

When the other witch finally looked up from the book, the judge's expression was inscrutable. "In the magical community, I suspect we don't publicize this fact because it's so rare that it might have people waiting all their lives for something they might never find." Mila blinked, confused, but the judge's next words couldn't have been clearer. "All right, here it is, Miss Bennet. Buckle up because I think you're in for a little shock."

Chapter Thirty

Uh-oh

RILEY

Riley was in his room, half-sitting, half-laying down on his dreadfully hard mattress while considering all the miserable choices that had caused him to sit here, alone in the dark, on this abominable piece of uncomfortable furniture instead of being wrapped up in Mila Bennet's soft, warm curves and her intoxicating coconut scent.

It was what was best for her, he repeated to himself for the millionth time. But the certainty of doing the honorable thing was a grim consolation prize and didn't make him feel any less miserable.

That was when a loud pounding started on his door.

Riley's first instinct was to reach for his stunner gun. He was about to unsheathe it when the pounding was joined by a woman's voice screaming. Mila's voice.

"Riley King, you'd better come to the door and let me in, or I'll blow it to smithereens. And then I won't just turn you into a toad. I'll turn you into a pet bunny and gift you to a pre-K school so that you will end your days having your tail pulled and with the screams of children in your bunny ears."

Riley had no idea what could've caused such animosity in the seemingly sweet witch he'd dropped home only a few hours earlier, but he thought it wise to get the door before she woke up the entire neighborhood.

He dropped the gun, useless against Mila, and pulled the black beanie over his head instead, a much more useful protective gear when it came to that particular witch.

When he opened the door, Riley found Mila on the other side, practically crackling with magic.

Her long hair was fanned behind her in a wide halo that seemed to float on a phantom wind, her eyes were glowing green, and actual sparks were coming out of the tip of her fingers.

Uh-oh.

Before Riley could have any reaction, she raised her hands and shoved him back into the house. Her palms and his chest never came in actual contact, but the force of her magic was enough to propel him halfway across his living room.

In a similar contact-free manner, Mila flipped her hand and the front door slammed shut with a wood-splintering bang.

Next, those phantom hands reached for the beanie atop his head, lifted it off him, and hurled it to the other side of the room. "You're not going to lie to me for this conversation."

Okay, now Riley was worried. Mila had been a bit of a firecracker from the first day they'd met, but the witch in front of him was a pissed-off, incandescent force of nature.

Still, in his career, he'd dealt with all kinds of formidable opponents, and he'd learned that sometimes the best way to respond to ferocious rage was with utter stillness.

So he shoved his hands into the pockets of his sweatpants and slowly tilted his head. "What are we fighting about?" he asked calmly.

A tornado wrecked the house in response as Mila started pacing the living room. "Still playing dumb, I see." She continued the pacing. "Anything you forgot to mention to me?"

Without the beanie on, Riley had to school his thoughts into very narrow tunnels. There were so many things he hadn't told her and right now he *could not* think about any of them.

Still, Mila could hear him loud and clear, and her response spared no punches. "I'm not talking about whatever other things you've failed to tell me. I want to know about the single, most important truth you've kept from me."

Oh, so she knew.

"Yes, I know, jackass," Mila spat, her voice angry, frustrated, and, worst of all, hurt. "We're hexing soulmates, and you were never going to tell me?"

Chapter Thirty-one

Hot Pursuit

RILEY

Riley stared at Mila, speechless. Somehow, hearing the words he'd been trying to escape since their first kiss being spoken out loud made everything worse, real, inevitable. They were soulmates.

The bond was as inescapable as Mila's rage.

"And you know what the worst part is?" she asked in that same hurt voice. "That if I hadn't found out on my own, you would've let me go on believing that this thing I feel inside"—she punched her chest for emphasis—"is fake, not real, the byproduct of a failed magical experiment."

Better than the alternative, Riley thought.

"What alternative?"

"Gargoyles." He grabbed the sides of his temples. "Can you stay out of my head for a second?"

"Why? So you can lie more easily?"

"I haven't lied to you." He tried to take

a step forward but found a wall of solid, angry air blocking him.

"A lie by omission is still a lie."

"Fine," Riley said, holding his hands up in surrender. "But can you at least listen to my side of the story? It's not as black and white as you're making it out to be."

Mila shifted her weight from foot to foot, considering his words. Finally, she nodded, and the magical barrier faded away. "Fine. Talk."

Riley took a deep breath and started pacing the room, needing movement to help organize his thoughts. "I didn't want to hurt you," he breathed. "I wanted to protect you."

"Protect me?" Mila's voice was incredulous. "By lying to me? By keeping the truth from me?"

Yeah, and he still did not know how she'd found out.

Mila narrowed her eyes at him. "Is that all you're worried about? How I found out?"

Riley's mind stood blank for a moment, but apparently, even that was wrong because next, Mila was marching toward the entrance door, shouting, "You know what? You get your wish. I'm out of here."

The door banged open for her, and Mila rushed out of his house just as furiously as she'd come in.

Riley ran after her, but by the time he reached the threshold, bracing against it with open arms, Mila was already straddling her broom.

One kick of her feet, and she was airborne, speeding away into the night.

Darn, stubborn witch.

In a blink, Riley grabbed his own broom and kicked off the ground in hot pursuit.

The chilly wind howled in his ears, and its icy fingers scraped against his cheeks as Riley chased after Mila. But he was too mad to even consider putting a warming spell around himself. He had only one aim in mind: to get to Mila and force her to land. A storm was cooking up, and this was no weather to fly into even under normal circumstances. Add that she was flustered and acting unreasonably, and Riley was really worried she could get hurt.

Even in the darkness, he could see Mila's silhouette, a small dot in the distance, but he pushed his broom to its limits and closed most of the gap between them.

"Stop!" he shouted over the wind, his

voice carrying a hint of desperation. "We need to talk about this!"

But his words must've gotten lost in the bellowing air currents because Mila didn't appear to have heard him.

Riley pushed his broom to the limits of what was sane and desperately yelled at her to stop. Only this time, he used his mind, not his voice.

Mila didn't slow down, but she turned back. *"There's nothing to talk about, Riley! You're a liar!"* came her telepathic response.

Riley gritted his teeth. *"I'm not a liar. I just didn't know how to tell you. And I thought you were better off not knowing, anyway. And slow down. You're going too fast. It's not safe."*

Mila scoffed and shook her head. *"Stop chasing me, and I'll slow down."*

Riley thought fast, trying to come up with something that would make her listen. *"Fine,"* he said finally. *"You want the truth? Here it is. Yes, we're soulmates. But that doesn't change anything between us."*

Mila braked, making her broom rear like a horse standing on its hind legs. She turned to face him, her eyes still brimming with anger. *"How can you even say that? Everything has changed!"*

Riley took a deep breath and looked at her, really looked at her. Even in the dim light of the moon, he could see the pain etched on her face, the hurt in her eyes, the tears streaming down her cheeks that had nothing to do with the cold wind whipping at them, and the way her hair floated around her face like a fiery red hurricane.

"Look, can we please talk about this when we are back on the ground?" he asked quietly. "It's not safe up here."

Riley guessed Mila had no intention of listening to him or following him to the safety of firm land by the way her eyes darted to the side, as if to gauge her best escape route.

Okay then, if reasoning with her didn't work, he'd have to go with Plan B.

Before Mila could move, Riley had already shifted the grip on his broom, putting it in attack mode. All magical law enforcement officers had brooms equipped with special assault gear that would allow them to capture a fleeing criminal.

One second before the magical net spread around Mila, her eyes widened. She'd probably gleaned his intentions from their mental bond. But it was too late. The green net of restraining power flashed out of his broom a second later and engulfed Mila, positively trapping her.

"Oh, you didn't." She trashed against the constraints. "You putrid eye of a zombie."

Now that she was safely in his custody, Riley made sure she was as comfortable as possible, then wrapped a warm blanket around the net.

Mila didn't appreciate it. "Keep your dirty aerial hands away from me, you ratty hair of an ogre. I hate you."

Riley ignored the protests and turned them back around toward his house. Throughout the brief journey, Mila screamed insults and threats at him that made being turned into a toad seem not the worst of fates.

He landed on his roof first, and then gently hovered Mila down. He unlatched the trapdoor he kept on his roof for emergency landings and pulled Mila flush to his chest. With a snap of his fingers, the net constraining her disappeared, and then they were falling through the hatch right back into his living room.

Chapter Thirty-two

No One Turned Up with Scales

MILA

Mila didn't know if it was the freefall that made her stomach soar or the fact that Riley had his arms wrapped around her as they fell.

But she didn't care because the moment they touched the ground, she started struggling against him. She tried to kick and punch and claw, but Riley was a hard wall of muscles who didn't give an inch. He kept her pressed against his chest with his strong arms, smothering her with his solid presence until the fight died out of Mila.

After she'd been limp in his arms for a few heartbeats, he started stroking her hair like he had earlier that morning on her porch. It had only been a few hours, and yet the world had changed, tilted on its axis, and toppled everything Mila believed in with it.

"Are you going to be good if I let you go?" Riley asked through their mental bond.

"Yes," Mila replied in the same way.

Honestly, she was too drained and exhausted to keep struggling.

Still, he kept her in his arms, kept stroking her hair in gentle caresses.

"You're not letting me go." She tentatively shot through the mental bond.

"I know," he replied.

Mila sighed and finally gave in to the instinct of snuggling even more into him. She buried her face into his neck and wrapped her arms around him.

He sighed. *"As first fights go, I think ours went pretty well."*

"How do you figure?"

"We're still standing. No one turned up green or with scales."

"There's still time for that."

The rumble of a low chuckle rolled up his chest.

"This isn't funny," Mila shot back.

"Sorry, I know."

She sniffled and looked up at him and spoke out loud for the first time since they'd re-entered the house. "You still haven't told me why? Why don't you want me?"

"Oh, Mila." The look of devastation on his face was heartbreaking. "You think that's why I didn't tell you? Because I don't want you?"

A wave of want so strong it shook her

very core, invaded her mind, her body, her very soul... but it wasn't hers. It was Riley's. This was how Riley felt about her.

Mila stared up at his beautiful, dark eyes. "If this is how you feel... why?"

Riley made a tortured face. "Nothing I'll ever say will make you understand."

"Then don't talk." She switched to using the mental bond again. *"Everything you feel, I can feel. Everything you remember, I can remember. Please, Riley, make me understand."*

Riley stared at her in utter stillness for so long she thought he was going to deny her. Then he cupped her cheek with one hand while keeping the other on the small of her back. He gave her a tiny nod and closed his eyes, dropping his forehead to hers.

And just like that, Mila wasn't in his living room anymore. She was outdoors on a dark night, her black boots plodding the frozen grass as she and her fellow magical special forces agents crossed carefully through the metal fence surrounding their target. On the other side of the fence, they swiftly crossed the wet pavement toward the back entrance of a warehouse.

Mila was seeing the world from about a head taller than what she was used to, and with every step, tension rose in her body until it was almost a palpable living thing. The low, squat building they had to breach was just up ahead and there was no room for mistakes; they had one chance at success and only seconds to complete the mission or fail trying.

The squad fanned out as soon as they reached their coordinates with stealthy precision, forming a defensive perimeter around the building while Mila and the team leader took the vanguard. Once everyone was in position, the squadron leader gave Mila the go-ahead to breach the door and, weirdly, she felt a surge of love and worry for him rise in her chest.

The enemy base camp, at first sight, seemed unguarded and deserted. Maybe their target had already left, or maybe he was such a powerful dark wizard that he didn't need any extra protection.

In a moment of quiet shame, Mila found herself hoping for the first option, but as soon as her hand touched the door handle, a heavy wave of magic hit her so hard she almost fell back. Then all hell broke loose.

The double entrance doors of the warehouse flew open, and all kinds of infernal creatures broke free. At once, all the wizards taking up the rearguard were engaged in battle with the demons, sparks of green and purple magic flying in all directions. Mila was about to join the fray when the agent she loved, the team leader, gave her a curt head-shake and directed her forward.

And then it was just the two of them inside the dark warehouse. They separated, circling the perimeter in opposite directions.

Mila had just passed a tall tower of crate boxes stacked one on top of the other when she heard a creaking noise behind her and, in a moment of blinding clarity, she understood she was no longer the hunter but had become the prey.

Mila spun around just as a bright purple blaze of light came at her. She dodged, rolling to the side. But the purple blasts kept on coming, and Mila was soon cornered, with nowhere left to escape. Just as fear seeped its way into Mila's heart, a figure completely clad in darkness flew out from one corner and aimed straight for her.

An unfamiliar feeling of terror raced through Mila's veins as she took in the dark wizard with his long cloak flapping behind him as he gathered magic in his hands and then shot it right at her chest. The last part of the memory had played in slow motion, but in reality, the attack mustn't have taken longer than a few seconds.

Mila closed her eyes, the fear of dying replaced by the knowledge she'd perish while carrying out her duty. She braced for an impact to the chest that never came. She only felt a searing pain in her left hip and then everything went dark.

The image swirled into a vortex of fog, and suddenly Mila was no longer in the warehouse and it wasn't night anymore. Pale orange strokes of pre-dawn were coloring the waking sky as Mila limped toward a black manor. The house was too tall and with too many turrets—one with a white eight-point star painted on it— hanging at weird angles to be standing. But there the house was, defying gravity and every law of nature. Mila found it familiar instead of odd.

She limped up the driveway, with a pain so dark and ugly swirling inside her it was burning a hole in her chest.

She made it to the door, the effort almost costing every last ounce of energy she'd left in her injured body. Still, she hesitated.

Mila knew what she had to do, but that didn't make it any easier. Taking ragged, agonizing breaths that left her throat raw, she knocked.

A woman perhaps in her fifties came to open the door. Mila loved her just as much as she'd loved the squadron leader—*loved*, past tense.

The woman took one look at Mila's face, their eyes met, and then the woman collapsed on the floor, howling. Harsh sounds of pain and rage, of despair and agony that left Mila's very soul shredded to pieces.

Slowly, the scene faded away, as did the cold. Warmth gradually seeped back into her bones as she returned to Riley's living room.

His eyes were wide open now, and he was staring at her. *"That,"* he said, and even if he was speaking mind to mind, the words still felt rough with anguish. *"That is how the wife of a chief inquisitor ends up, with her heart torn out of her chest and her soul shattered into a million pieces."* He gently stroked the side of her face, tucking her hair behind her ear. *"It's the last thing I would want for you."*

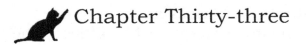 # Chapter Thirty-three

Love Me Like You Do

MILA

"Was the squadron leader your father?"

"He was Chief Inquisitor before me." Riley gave her a curt nod, his entire face contorting with pain and regret. *"He jumped in front of the blast, taking the hit for me while also delivering the killing shot to the dark wizard we were chasing. All I got was a graze to the hip."*

"Oh, Riley. I'm so sorry." She hugged him tightly, burying her face once again into the nook of his shoulder.

Riley squeezed her as if he was allowing himself a moment of weakness, but then he went rigid again in her arms and kept talking through the mental bond. *"That's why I can't have anyone fall in love with me. It wouldn't be fair to them. It wouldn't be fair to you."*

Mila let out a bitter chortle in her head. *"Sorry to break it to you, Chief Inquisitor King, but it might be a little too late for that."*

Riley didn't respond to her in words. Maybe re-living the death of his father had left him even more open and vulnerable than he already was, but as he tangled his fingers in her hair next, Mila was literally flooded with love.

The emotion was identical to the one already swelling in her chest, but feeling also his side of it made their love almost unbearable.

"I should take you home," Riley whispered.

"What?" Mila pulled back. "You still don't want to pursue this?" A fear, dark and all-consuming, worse than the one Riley had experienced facing death, reared its head inside Mila's chest. "Riley, I literally just felt how you feel about me. You can't be serious."

"Mila we can't, *I* can't. I can't be on the job every day terrorized of what it'd do to you if something happened to me."

The words cut deep. She took a step back, slipping out of his arms and gasping for air. "Riley, you can't shut yourself off from love. You deserve to feel loved and to give love in return."

Riley's eyes were dark and unfathomable as he stared back at her. "Love comes with a cost, Mila. You saw what happened to my mom. I can't let that happen to you."

Mila shook her head, determination setting in. "Yeah, your mother became a widow young, too young. But, Riley, I bet that if you asked your mom if she could have that pain pulled free of her at the price of never having loved your dad, she'd say no."

Riley's mouth quirked up into a small smile. "She *would* say no."

"Exactly," Mila said, taking a step closer. "Love is worth the risk, Riley. You can't let fear control your life and emotions."

"I don't know how to do that," he whispered, his voice barely audible over the pounding of Mila's heart in her chest.

"Take a chance with me," she said, reaching out to intertwine her fingers with his. "Let me love you."

Riley's gaze softened, and he brought their joined hands to his lips, kissing her knuckles softly. "That's not the problem; I can't let you—"

"No," Mila interrupted him. "What you *can't* do is decide for me. If I still want to date a magical law enforcement agent, even after knowing all the risks, it's my choice. The only decision *you* can make here is if you want to love *me*."

Riley looked at her, a battle raging behind his dark irises. When his jaw settled into a hard, unforgiving line, Mila was sure she'd lost. But then his face assumed the most tortured look of the night, and letting out a frustrated groan, he closed the distance between them.

His hands went to cup her cheeks while his mouth crashed onto hers. The kiss was equally desperate and tender, filled with all the longing and fear they'd both been holding back. Mila's heart was pounding so hard that she was almost dizzy, but she felt alive like she never had before. She clung to Riley, kissing him back just as fiercely as he was kissing her, melting into his embrace, feeling every inch of his body pressed against hers.

The tension in his shoulders slowly relaxed as he deepened the kiss, exploring every corner of her mouth with a feverish need.

Riley's hands moved from her face, slowly and deliberately tracing the contours of her body. No, not just his human hands, but his aerial ones as well, until Mila felt like every inch of her body was being cherished and caressed by him. Electric sparks traveled up and down every nerve in her body each time his fingers—flesh or air—grazed against her skin.

Yet, it wasn't enough. When Riley started trading gentle bites mixed with kisses down her neck, Mila felt like she was about to explode with pleasure. But she captured his mouth with hers once again, kissing him like she never wanted to stop.

And maybe Riley didn't want her to ever stop either, because he moaned loudly into her mouth, and pulled her up into his arms until she was seated on the back of the couch, her legs wrapped around his waist and their bodies almost fused together.

Now Riley started trailing butterfly kisses from her lips down her jaw as he slipped his hands underneath the fabric of her sweater, his fingers exploring her naked skin. The light touches slowly morphed into needy, possessive caresses.

It was sweet agony, and Mila never wanted it to end.

The kiss seemed to last an eternity, but when they pulled away from each other, gasping for air, Riley rested his forehead against hers. They stayed locked together like that while resting their foreheads against one another's, taking a moment to process what had just happened between them—or at least Mila was.

"I can't promise it won't be hard," he breathed out. "But I do want to love you."

His eyes were the clearest she had ever seen them, no fear or regret hiding there now, only a burning plea for understanding that nearly made her cry out with its intensity.

Mila smiled softly, feeling tears well up in her eyes. "That's all I could ever ask for."

They stayed like that for a few more moments, simply holding each other, until Riley finally kissed her again.

Tender at first, then with renewed passion. When he almost pushed her over the couch in his quest to keep their bodies flush, he pulled back.

"Maybe we should move this to my bedroom," he said.

"That sounds like a great idea," Mila half-chuckled, half-whispered, breathless with need and aching with desire.

He scooped her up and carried her bride-style down the hallway to his bedroom, gracefully dropping her on the hard mattress while still cradling her, looking down her body like it was the best gift he'd ever received.

But then his eyes darkened, and it became clear he wanted more, that the clothes covering her had become his enemy.

With a wicked smirk, Riley let his aerial hands do the dirty work, and Mila's jeans began to unbutton and unzip as if by magic—well, by *actual* magic. Those wicked hands were already pulling her pants down her legs, while Riley never stopped kissing her.

Mila had no trouble following suit. She sunk her hands under his sweatshirt and helped him pull it over his head.

Now they were both undressing each other, hands fumbling over buttons and zippers as they kissed and bit each other's lips, mouths, and throats.

When their bodies finally came in contact, Mila felt like she might burn from the inside out with pleasure. The feverishly light touches Riley was tracing all over her body were sweet torture of the best kind, but she needed more.

She needed him.

"Please, Riley," she begged him, her fingers digging into his silky hair. And then, when she thought she would explode with agony if he kept denying her, Riley pulled her back from her trance.

"Look at me," he ordered.

She did. He stood still over her for an unbearably long instant, and then finally gave her what she craved: their bodies were joined just as their souls would be for all eternity.

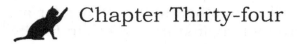 Chapter Thirty-four

We Should Fight More Often

MILA

A long time later, Riley sagged on the mattress next to her. He turned his face on the pillow to face Mila, and with the goofiest smile, he said, "We should fight more often."

Mila burst out laughing. There was so much joy inside her she felt too small to contain it. She beamed at him with an equally dorky face. "If you're prepared to admit how wrong you are every time we fight, I'm down for it."

Riley grabbed her by the waist and pulled her toward himself, rolling half on top of her while simultaneously tickling her sides and nuzzling her neck. "You're getting cocky."

Mila giggled uncontrollably and couldn't even come up with a smart comeback.

"As if you could talk, Mr. Smug Grin," she managed to choke out at last.

"Oh, I *am* smug." Riley's steadily growing smirk was glued to his face. "I have the most beautiful witch in Salem in my bed."

Mila mock-gagged. "Now you're just being corny."

"Who did you call corny?"

Mila couldn't help but laugh when he started tickling her even more. He wasn't listening to her pleas to stop, so Mila had to resort to more subtle techniques. She shifted under him so that now he wasn't only half on top of her, but squarely between her legs.

It didn't take long for Riley to catch up. He stopped tickling her but was still grinning like an idiot when he said, "Seriously, Bennet, you'd resort to seducing me?"

In the most innocent voice she could muster, Mila replied, "The tactic seems to be working, Inquisitor King."

Using his formal title finally did it. Riley's pupils blew out and tickling became the furthest thing on his mind.

Mila didn't mind the shift of focus one bit.

***

Another long while later, thoroughly exhausted from the re-match under the sheets, Mila lay on the mattress, facing Riley and smiling slightly deliriously for a while before he suddenly got up and put a shirt on.

Mila thought that covering his six-pack was a crime against all women.

He smirked and shot her a quick, *"Heard that,"* through the mental bond.

"Oh, well," she shot back. *"It's true."*

"How come I can hear you, too, now?"

She smiled and stretched under the sheets like a lazy cat. *"I guess all the sex loosened my mental barriers."*

He laughed, both out loud and through their mental connection. "I promise I'm getting dressed for an excellent reason," Riley said, pulling on a pair of sweatpants that hung low on his hips—gargoyles, even his hipbones were so sexy, as was that V of muscles disappearing below his waistband.

Looking at her from under a curtain of black hair, Riley buttoned down the shirt and covered all that deliciousness.

Mila groaned in protest in her head.

"Steaming cauldrons, Bennet, you're a greedy little goblin."

She sat on the bed and grabbed him by those delicious hips to pull him to her. "Can you tell me again what is this excellent reason you have to be getting dressed? Because at the moment, I really can't fathom a single one."

"Can I interest you in having dinner with me, Bennet?" he said, pressing a soft kiss to Mila's temple. "Or did you eat already?"

"No, I came here straight from the DMJ."

"The DMJ?" Riley frowned.

"Yeah, that's how I found out we're soulmates... Judge Templeton figured it out after I told her about the mental bond."

"Why did you tell her about it?"

"I was trying to convince her my potion must've somehow still worked on us after she'd educated me on magical law enforcement officers wearing protective gear against curses, and stunner gun hits, removing all magic from their target."

Riley tilted his neck and scratched the back of his head, visibly embarrassed. "Sorry about that. I really thought you'd be better off without me."

Mila squeezed him possessively. "Never."

"Why did you go to see Judge Templeton in the first place, anyway?"

"To ask her to assign me to a different community service."

"I thought you loved working on the case."

"I did, but..." Mila left the sentence hanging.

"Then it was because of me." An affirmation, not a question.

"Yes, because even when I thought it was all fake, it was unbearable to be near you feeling what I was feeling and not being able to..." When words failed Mila, she grabbed his hand and laced their fingers together

He flashed her a sheepish grin, raising an eyebrow suggestively, and finished the sentence for her. "Not being able to do everything that we just did."

Mila blushed, and he teased her relentlessly, "Oh, Bennet, I find it so cute you choose to blush now."

She stood up from the bed and playfully slapped his shoulder. "I didn't choose to, and stop teasing me or I'll really turn you into a toad."

He made a mock-serious tone. "Mmm, I'm not sure toads have sexy hipbones though."

She swatted him again. "You're the worst." Then she got serious. "Anyway, it wasn't just the physical part—or the absence of it—that was unbearable." She looked up at him. "It was, ridiculous as it may sound after only three days, not being allowed to tell you I love you."

His eyes snatched hers and got so hexing intense. "I love you, too."

"I know that now, but before... I was thinking this feeling so strong and all-consuming I had inside of me wasn't real... or that it was wrong, or that I'd forced you into feeling something similar when you couldn't stand me—"

Her speech was cut off by him cupping her cheek and hugging her close to his chest. He smelled delicious, like wind and snow and fabric softener and her favorite cologne.

"I'm sorry," Riley apologized. "Mila Bennet, you're the best thing that's ever happened to me, and I've been an idiot."

"Yeah," Mila agreed. "A rude, grumpy, sexy idiot. But you're *my* idiot now, so stop moping and go make me dinner."

She smiled up at him, teasing.

He kissed her forehead again and walked out of the bedroom. "You get away with ordering me around only because of all the sex."

Mila sank back on the bed, still grinning like a total dork, and consoled herself by ogling his butt as he exited the room.

"Also heard that," Riley called from the hallway.

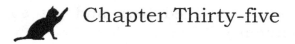 Chapter Thirty-five

Spoon Me All Night Long

RILEY

Seated at his kitchen table, Riley watched Mila scarf down the homemade pizza he'd prepared for dinner like she hadn't eaten in days, and found he couldn't stop smiling.

He hadn't felt this happy since, well, if he had to be honest, since before his father had died. And it was all because of her. This beautiful witch who currently had tomato sauce dripping down her chin from the corner of her mouth.

Riley couldn't resist. He reached out, wiped the smudge with his thumb, and then sucked it.

Mila stared at him, half-captivated, half-mock-outraged. "You have to stop eating food off my face."

"Why?"

"It's gross."

"It's not."

"It's the grossest."

Riley rolled his eyes. "I already see you're going to be a difficult soulmate."

Mila all-out laughed at that. "That we

might agree on."

Riley grabbed a napkin to wipe the rest of Mila's face. "But I already know I'm going to enjoy every minute of it."

She flung her arms around his shoulders and side-hugged him. "Me, too. Especially if you keep making homemade pizza. I would've never pegged you down as a chef. What else can you make?"

"I'm a thirty-five-year-old wizard who's been living alone for almost twenty years. I can cook most things."

Now Mila shifted fully onto his lap. "First, you're so old."

"Hey." He playfully pinched her butt.

Mila squealed and laughed. "And second, you have a spell-oven, don't you?"

He narrowed his eyes in mock severity. "I. Do. Not."

Mila jumped off of him and rushed to the stove. "So, if I open this door now." She pointed at the oven. "I will find a simple, human oven."

Riley crossed his arms over his chest. "Go ahead."

Mila did and squealed even harder when she confirmed it was no magic appliance that had made dinner. "Oh, sparkling gargoyles." She turned around to face him and circled a hand toward him. "You look like that and you can even cook? I think my swoon rate just increased by sixty-four percent from that fact alone." Mila's eyebrow raised suggestively. "So... what's on the menu for dessert?"

Riley closed the space between them and pressed her back against the kitchen counter. "What would you want? I have a pretty wide range of *specialties...*"

Mila pressed her palms flat on his chest, but without pushing him away. "Riley, I'm already swooning. You don't need to seduce me further."

Riley smiled at that, wickedly, and he snapped his fingers, causing all the kitchen lights to dim considerably, leaving them in a cozy, suffused atmosphere. Her eyes glittered with amusement under the new light as Riley trailed lazy kisses up her collarbone.

"Are you sure about that? Because I love seducing you. I love you."

Mila whimpered. She wrapped her arms tightly around his neck and pulled him closer, their bodies fitting together perfectly. "If you seduce me any harder, I might blow up and become stardust," she breathed against his lips. "Nice trick the lights, by the way."

She bit his lower lip in a way that

drove him insane. In response, Riley's lips met hers in a fiery kiss.

Their bodies molded together, and the heat between them intensified with each passing second. Mila let out a moan as Riley's hands traveled down to her waist, pulling her closer to him.

As their lips continued their sweet torture, Riley's magic swirled around them, wrapping them in a warm cocoon of energy. Then their kisses grew more passionate, skin searing as their hands roamed over each other's bodies. Riley lifted Mila onto the kitchen counter, pulling away only to shed their clothes as quickly as possible. The lights flickered over their naked skin as they surrendered to each other, desire and love mingling in a heady mix until they were both truly spent. So much so, that when Riley carried Mila baby-koala-style to bed, she fell asleep in his arms halfway down the hall. He lovingly dropped her onto the mattress and kissed the top of her head as he pulled the covers snugly over her. "Sweet dreams, my love."

Then he climbed into bed next to her and spooned her all night.

Chapter Thirty-six

The Early Bird Gets the Killer

MILA

The next morning, pixies fluttered in Mila's belly before she was even fully conscious. Then she blinked and realized she was in love. With Riley, her soulmate. She turned and found him snuggled close to her, his face buried in her hair, his muscular arms wrapped over her waist.

A wave of powerful emotions hit her again: love, happiness, longing, excitement... For the first time in a long while, Mila couldn't wait to live her life. With him, her soulmate. Her sexy, kind, good in the kitchen, and even greater in bed soulmate.

That's when Riley cracked an eyelid open. "Gargoyles, Bennet, you're swooning so hard you woke me!"

"Oh, really? As if you could speak, Inquisitor King. Is that a magic wand in your pocket, or are you really happy to see me?"

He pinned her hands over her head and rolled on top of her. "Sassy right from the early hours, I see."

Mila loved the way he looked at her as if she was the center of his universe. "That a problem, Inquisitor King?"

"Not in the slightest." He kissed her, slow and languid, and then did many other things to her...

***

Afterward, Mila was about ready to go back to sleep when Riley surprised her by slowly but methodically shoving her out of bed.

"Hey, what are you doing?" she protested. She barely had enough strength left in her limbs to lie down peacefully, let alone keep upright.

"I'm making you get up."

"Why?"

"Well, in case you had forgotten, Bennet, we still have a murder case to solve."

She bit her lower lip. "Can't we do it after eleven?" She needed at least three more hours of sleep after the night—and the morning—they had.

"Sorry, but the early bird gets the killer."

"You're awful," she complained, finally stumbling to her feet—stark naked, right in front of him.

His eyes were a vortex of darkness as he took her in.

Mila smirked, satisfied. "If you could direct me to the shower, Inquisitor King, I'd happily get ready for work."

He had a wolf-like expression as he leaped off the bed and scooped her up into his arms. "Let me help you with that, Miss Bennet."

Riley carried her to the bathroom, turned on the shower, and then did even more unspeakable things to her while he washed her up, which made standing afterward all the more difficult.

"I think you've melted all the bones in my body," Mila complained as she got dressed in her clothes from the night before.

"We can't have that." He dropped a soft kiss on her still bare shoulder. "Come on, I have the perfect remedy to make bones grow back."

"Really? Like what?" Mila asked skeptically. She was pretty positive her invertebrate status was permanent.

"Why? Coffee and donuts." He flashed her that ridiculous grin of his again.

Mila shook her head. "Stop that or I'm never recovering from all the swooning."

***

They drove to the coffee shop in his car, and then, after breakfast, they went back to Mr. MacNeil's house. But the silver fox once again wasn't home, so they prepared themselves for another long stakeout.

Only today, the prospect wasn't as gloomy as the day before. In fact, Mila enjoyed having plenty of time to do nothing other than talk to Riley, getting to know him—and okay, they might've smuggled the occasional kiss in there, too. They spoke about everything, from their families, to their childhoods, their dreams and fears, and everything in between.

As they moved on to discussing the present, Mila had a hard time explaining her lack of a clear direction in her career and why she kept hopping between this or that temp job with the local witching agency and couldn't find her true calling. And the relief she felt when Riley didn't judge her for it almost felt overwhelming.

"If it helps," he said. "I think you're a darn spectacular detective."

Mila crossed her eyes. "You say that only because you want me to join the force and become the literal boss of me."

"Nah," he said, dead serious, "you'd be too much of a pain in the ass to supervise."

"Hey." She mock-punched him.

He caught her wrist before she could punch him again and held on to her a little too long. "And your stubbornness is just one of the many things I love about you."

Mila squeezed his hand back. "Same here."

The air between them thickened, and it looked like they were about to smuggle in another one of those stolen kisses when Riley's phone rang.

"It's Sarah Michelle," he said, checking his screen. "I have to pick up."

Mila nodded.

"Inquisitor King."

And gargoyles, if the tone of authority in which he said his title didn't make her toes curl into her shoes. Every. Single. Time.

Riley shot her a look, signaling he probably heard that last mental comment but needed to concentrate on the conversation he was having.

Mouthing a low "sorry," Mila propped up her mental barriers and let Riley finish the call without interrupting with more naughty distractions.

After not long, Riley hung up and turned to her, already putting the car into gear. "The doctors are waking up Mrs.

Blackwell in a few hours." He pulled off the road, making a U-turn in the hospital's direction. "At this point, we might as well wait for Mrs. Blackwell to regain consciousness and ask her who gave her the poisoned cupcake."

"You think she'll remember? After being knocked out for so long?"

"We can only hope she does."

The hospital was only ten minutes away, and in the car, Riley filled her in on the details of Mrs. Blackwell's condition that Agent Callidora had related to him on the phone.

Once they reached the hospital, Mila shivered when she opened the door to get out of Riley's car. No matter how many layers she put on, winter in Massachusetts would always be too cold for her. The frigid December air swirled in around them and enveloped them in an icy embrace that almost made her teeth chatter, at least until Riley swooped in and put his warm air blanket over her while escorting her to the entrance with an arm slung on the small of her back.

And suddenly, the cold winter day didn't seem so harsh anymore.

Inside the hospital, the atmosphere was the opposite. Impossibly warm and stuffy. Mila peeled off her coat while Riley walked up to the reception desk to confirm the exact time of Mrs. Blackwell's reawakening.

They still had a couple of hours. Nonetheless, they went up to Mrs. Blackwell's hospital room to give Sarah Michelle a break from her guard duties and were utterly surprised to find Mr. MacNeil seated by the bed, lovingly holding the patient's hand over the covers. So maybe Jacob Sheridan was right and there was nothing between Mr. MacNeil and Mrs. Knox and MacNeil really was Mrs. Blackwell's new secret lover.

"Definitely not the attitude of a killer," Mila shot down the mental bond.

Riley shrugged. *"Could he be drowning in regret?"*

Mila rolled her eyes. *"Cynical much?"*

"Let's ask him a few questions, and we'll see."

Mila nodded, and they entered the room.

Once Sarah Michelle had gone, Riley flashed his badge to Mr. MacNeil. He was so hot when he showed his badge that Mila was half tempted to ask him for a little role-play that night.

He shot her one of his chastising looks. *"I'm trying to do a job here, Bennet."*

"Sorry." She made a zipper-over-mouth gesture and promised to be good over the mental bond.

"Mr. MacNeil," Riley continued in his sexy detective voice. "Would you mind answering a few questions for us?"

"Not at all, Detective."

"This is the second time we've run into you here. Are you and Mrs. Blackwell especially close?"

"Yes," the poor, old man sighed. "We are in love."

Riley nodded. "But your relationship wasn't public knowledge, am I correct?"

"No. She had recently broken up with Jacob and wanted to spare his feelings."

"I see, so your relationship was in a good place, no resentments, no recent fights?"

"Detective King, if you're asking me if I'd ever hurt my Josephine, the answer is no." There was a note of disdain in the man's voice that made him sound even more truthful.

"Mr. MacNeil," Mila jumped in. "Sorry for asking, but you and Mrs. Knox seemed pretty close the other day. Has there ever been something romantic between the two of you?"

"With Cherry? No, we've always been just friends. I mean, she's been very supportive since Josephine took ill, but that's it."

"Supportive how, Mr. MacNeil, if you don't mind me asking?" Mila prodded.

"Oh, she's been cooking me meals, helping out with groceries too, and she insisted on accompanying me to the hospital every single time I came."

Riley shot her a look. *"Where are you getting at with this?"*

"I can't put my finger on it just yet, but I'm sure there's something more to it."

"But she didn't come today?" Mila asked, out loud this time.

"Cherry was here earlier, but when the doctor told us they were going to wake up Josephine in a few hours and I decided to wait, she said she had to go home." There was a heartbeat of silence, and then Mr. MacNeil added, "Something about packing."

Mila's heart pounded, and she sought Riley's eyes.

"What?" he asked through the bond.

"Don't you see? Cherry Knox is the poisoner."

He crossed his arms over his chest, very much the skeptical inquisitor.

Mila rolled her eyes. *"Okay, hear me out, Chief. What I think happened is that Cherry Knox is secretly in love with Mr.*

MacNeil—"

"And how'd you reach that conclusion?"

"It's just a strong vibe I got from the way she was behaving the other day when we ran into them. I thought they were a couple."

"Yeah, me too."

"And Sheridan confirmed she'd love to sink her claws into MacNeil. So, she's in love with him, but then she somehow finds out that MacNeil is already secretly dating Mrs. Blackwell."

"And she decides to take out the completion?"

"Exactly, and be his shoulder to cry on."

Riley looked excited now. "But things didn't go according to plan, did they?"

"No, because my love potion saved Mrs. Blackwell."

"Wait, wait." Riley frowned. "If she's the poisoner, why wait so long to flee? The doctors always said Mrs. Blackwell was going to wake up, eventually."

"Maybe she thought Mrs. Blackwell would still kick the bucket while in the hospital." Mila shrugged. "But if she was here when the doctors announced they'd wake her today. Mrs. Knox probably panicked and decided to flee before being *pointed at as the poisoner."*

"Flee where? Isn't she a little old to be a criminal on the run?"

"I've no idea. Let's see if Mr. MacNeil knows." Mila switched to speaking aloud. "I'm sorry, Mr. MacNeil. Did Mrs. Knox say where she was going?"

"Yeah, she said something about booking a last-minute cruise."

"A cruise to where?"

"Mexico, I think."

"No-extradition Mexico, uh?" Mila shot to Riley quietly before adding aloud, "Thanks, Mr. MacNeil. We'll see you later."

"Right." Riley nodded. *"Let's see if we can catch this adorable old lady-killer before she leaves the country."*

Chapter Thirty-seven

Poker Face

RILEY

Riley and Mila left the hospital in a hurry, determined to catch Mrs. Knox before she got away. They hopped into Riley's car and drove at breakneck speed through town toward Cherry Knox's house.

When they reached their destination, Riley wasted no time. He killed the engine of his car and vaulted out, not even waiting for Mila as he speed-walked up Mrs. Knox's driveway. In a few long strides, he was already at the front door and knocking. He had to pound on the door multiple times before the tired and suspicious-looking old woman opened it, holding a suitcase in her hands.

"Oh," Mrs. Knox reeled in surprise. "I thought it was my taxi. Who are you, young man?" she asked, and Riley couldn't shake the feeling that despite her playing dumb, she'd recognized him as the police detective from the hospital all too well.

It was in the way her shrewd, beady eyes darted to the side as if to search for an escape route.

"Detective King, and this is my partner, Detective Bennet." Riley flashed his human-confounding badge. "I need to speak to you about the attempted murder of Mrs. Blackwell."

Mrs. Knox's eyes widened in surprise. "What? I had nothing to do with that!"

"Then you won't have trouble answering a few questions," Mila said, stepping forward.

Mrs. Knox backed away, her hand clutching a suitcase tightly. "I'm sorry, Detectives, but I really don't have the time now. I was about to leave." She lifted the suitcase as a demonstration. "My taxi will be here anytime."

"Then we have time to talk until it *gets* here," Riley said, subtly putting a shield on the house so that they wouldn't be disturbed even if Mrs. Knox's getaway car did arrive.

"That's ridiculous!" Mrs. Knox exclaimed, her voice turning shrill.

"Is it?" Riley asked. "We spoke with Mr. MacNeil, and he mentioned you were very supportive of him during his visits to the hospital."

Mrs. Knox's eyes darted back and forth. "I was just being kind."

"And then there's the fact that you

conveniently left when Mrs. Blackwell was about to be woken up from her coma," Mila added.

"I have a flight to catch!" Mrs. Knox protested.

"A flight to Mexico for New Year's?" Riley asked pointedly.

Mrs. Knox hesitated for a fraction of a second before quickly regaining her composure. "Yes, that's correct. Last I checked, going on vacation is not a crime."

"Interesting," Riley said with a raised eyebrow. "And what do you plan on doing once you get there? Living out your days on a beach somewhere sipping margaritas?"

Mrs. Knox glared at him but remained tight-lipped.

"Mrs. Knox," Riley continued. "I strongly encourage you to cooperate."

"Detectives, I know my rights, so unless you have a warrant or are here to arrest me, I'd kindly ask you to leave."

"Very well, Mrs. Knox, you leave us no choice." Riley conjured a search warrant out of thin air and drove it out of his coat pocket, handing it to a stunned-into-silence Mrs. Knox.

At the sight of the official paper, the old lady looked flustered and started fidgeting with her suitcase, but reluctantly accepted defeat and opened up her home for them to look around.

Riley quickly surveyed the area, making a show of searching through cupboards and drawers while he weaved a searching spell that would guide him toward what he was looking for, even if Riley still didn't know what it was.

He released the spell and waited for the magic to tug him in the right direction. Soon, the pull came, and Riley followed it to the kitchen, where the magic guided him to a set of potted plants on the windowsill. One among them in particular.

Bingo.

Riley lifted the plant and turned to Mrs. Knox. "This is a castor oil plant, Mrs. Knox, whose beans are used to make ricin poison, the same poison that almost killed Mrs. Blackwell."

He thought he had the old lady nailed down, but she simply shrugged. "It's just a plant. It's not illegal to have one. If this is all the evidence you have, you don't have a case."

"She's not wrong," Mila said telepathically.

"So what? We keep her here until Mrs. Blackwell wakes up and identifies her as

the killer."

"What if Mrs. Blackwell doesn't remember anything? We have to nail her now."

"How?"

"Let me try something," Mila said, and Riley recognized the knitting of magic in the way she moved her fingers.

Then Mila's phone started ringing.

She picked up, putting on a show worthy of an Oscar.

"Yes? Did she wake up? Yes, we're here now... and she's sure, beyond the shade of a doubt? Thank you, Sarah Michelle. No, we'll take care of it. Reinforcement won't be needed."

Then Mila, with the most serious poker face he'd ever seen, turned toward Mrs. Knox and said, "It's over, Mrs. Knox. Josephine Blackwell just woke up and identified you as the person who delivered the poisoned cupcake to her."

For a moment, Mrs. Knox kept still, her eyes darting around the room as if she was still planning to make a run for it. But then the old lady took one look at them, at him in particular, Riley noted, and she must have decided there was no reality in which she could outrun them.

Mrs. Knox finally gave up and started confessing, telling them about how Mrs.

Blackwell was a man-eater who would only use George and then discard him once she'd tired of him, just as she'd done to poor Jacob. While she truly loved MacNeil and would've done anything for him—including killing someone.

With the confession, the case was truly solved and could finally be handed down to the regular Salem PD. Riley called the local human authorities, and they led away a handcuffed Mrs. Knox into a police car with flashing lights.

Riley and Mila watched them drive away from the curb in front of the old lady's house until the human police vehicle disappeared behind a corner.

"Well, that was intense," Riley said, turning to Mila.

"Goblins, it was. The dating scene of septuagenarians is cutthroat," she replied with a smirk. "I can't believe she actually did it."

"Yeah, me neither." Riley paused for a moment before adding, "But I have to admit, you were pretty impressive back there with the fake phone call and beautiful poker face, especially since Sarah Michelle just called and informed me that Mrs. Blackwell couldn't remember a thing about the night of the recital."

Mila's eyes widened. "Is Mrs. Blackwell all right?"

"As well as could be expected given the recent poisoning."

Now Mila's expression turned wicked as she grabbed him by the lapels of his coat. "Does that mean you're officially off the clock, Inquisitor King?"

Riley smirked, relishing the feeling of her hands on him. "I suppose it does. What do you have in mind, Miss Bennet?"

Mila leaned in close, her lips almost touching his ear. "I think it's time for a little celebration."

 # Chapter Thirty-eight

Epilog

RILEY

A year later, on Christmas Eve

Chief Inquisitor Riley King killed the engine of his black sedan and sighed as he picked up a bouquet of vervain flowers, briar shrubs, and a handful of sorry-I'm-late-for-Christmas-Eve-dinner-Mom from the passenger seat.

Then he switched the bouquet to his other arm and picked up a second bouquet made of holly, sage, and sorry-I'm-late-for-Christmas-Eve-dinner-my-beloved-wife.

He locked his car and crossed the street toward Chiron Manor, his mother's house, noting the usual number of violations to the Conformism Act of 1792 as he walked up the driveway. He really would have to give his mom a pep talk about it one day or another. But for now, Riley filed the thought away as a New Year's resolution.

He was about to ring the bell when the door flew open, and Mila threw her arms around him, lacing her fingers behind his neck.

For a moment, he wondered how she'd known he had arrived, but soon got distracted by her soft body pressed against his hard one.

Mila smiled, and without uttering a word, she told him. *"I could hear your grumpy commentary up the driveway from a mile away."*

Before he could respond, she pulled him in for a kiss like she did whenever he got home at night.

With both his hands busy holding flowers, Riley had to resort to other means of hugging his wife.

He called to his magic and bent the icy winter air to his will, turning it into a pair of warm aerial hands, which he employed to cup his wife's very shapely behind.

Mila laughed against his mouth and pulled back. "Oh, naughty, Inquisitor King."

Riley shrugged. "What can I say? I missed you, Bennet."

She flashed him a sultry grin before taking the bouquets from his arms. "I missed you, too. Come on, let's go inside."

They entered the house, the scent of cinnamon and pine immediately hitting Riley's nose. Mila led him into the dining room where his mother had already prepared two glass vases filled with water to hold the flowers.

That was the thing about having a powerful seer for a mother and a powerful witch for a wife. They didn't let you get away with anything.

Riley chuckled as he took a seat at the dining table. The table was decorated with a red and green tablecloth with matching napkins, plates, and silverware. A large centerpiece made of pine cones, holly leaves, and candles sat in the middle of the table. And this year, instead of the usual three plates, the table was set for five, Mila and her familiar being the latest additions to the family dinner.

Mila's talking cat, Abel—or Abby, as he detested to be called by Riley—was a feisty little ball of fur with a lot of opinions. And while he and Riley would probably never be BFFs, they shared their love and support for Mila, which made their cohabitation bearable.

And at least the cat was Myron's new favorite target at all family celebrations, shifting the raccoon's petty attention away from Riley.

Glenda came in from the kitchen, holding the traditional crisped turkey in her hands. She dropped the roasted bird in the center of the table and then turned to Riley, kissing him on the cheek.

"Mom." He pulled her into a side hug. "Sorry I'm late."

She arched an eyebrow. "Work again?"

Riley braced himself, mentally preparing himself for Glenda's reprimands.

"Don't be too hard on your mom," Mila mentally chided him from the other side of the table, sporting a mock-serious frown. *"She means well."*

Riley didn't have time to respond before Glenda, right on script, sighed and shook her head while she started cutting the turkey. "You work too much, Riley. You should spend more time with your beautiful wife." His mom turned to Mila now. "Maybe he should join you in the private sector. You could work together."

In the past year, Mila had gone back to being a Magical PI and opened her own agency.

"And let me guess." Riley smiled charmingly. "Start making as many witchlings as possible."

Mila hid her smirk behind a cup of moonlight mead and, mischievous eyes fixed on him, teased him silently. *"Hey, I don't mind the witchlings-making activity one bit, Inquisitor King."*

Mila knew that using his formal title drove him mad with desire, and she did it whenever they were in public and she was safe from the consequences.

"Oh, I don't mind the consequences either," she shot back. *"In fact, I'm wearing an early Christmas present for you, my love."*

She shot him a mental image of herself staring in the mirror while wearing a red lace lingerie set.

Riley's eyes bugged. *"You're wearing that right now?"*

"Yep, and I can't wait to get home and for you to unwrap me, Inquisitor King."

Riley let out a frustrated groan in his head, and Mila burst out laughing.

Glenda paused her carving of the turkey and studied them. "Are you teasing each other again over that mental bond of yours?"

Riley and Mila lowered their gazes guiltily.

"Well," Glenda continued. "I say less flirting and more doing 'cause I want grandwitchlings and—"

"I'm not getting any younger," Riley, Mila, Myron, and Abel all finished the sentence for Glenda in chorus.

Which made all of them burst out

laughing, Glenda included.

As the last of the laughter died down, Glenda served them, and they began to eat the Christmas feast.

A sense of profound contentment washed over Riley as he ate the savory turkey and sipped the moonlight mead. He was surrounded by the people he loved, and there was no place he'd rather be. When he looked at Mila, the twinkle in her eyes told him she felt the same way.

He couldn't believe that merely a year ago he hadn't known her, that they'd been strangers, and that—

"You were about to stun me with your big *gun?"* she interrupted, through the mental bond.

"For the millionth time, I didn't stun you."

"No, right, you were happy just scooping me up from the tub and admiring my gorgeous naked body and loooong mermaid hair."

"Yes, but that was before you started talking." Riley grinned.

Mila rolled her eyes playfully.

Riley admired his wife with unabashed adoration for a few long seconds. *"But seriously, Bennet, you're the best gift I could've ever asked for."*

Her eyes got so big.

"Are you swooning over there, Bennet?"

"Just a little."

"Good, because I, too, can't wait to go home and unwrap you," he shot down the bond and then winked at his wife.

MILA

Mila slid into the passenger seat of Riley's sleek black sedan, the leather cool against the back of her thighs through the thin nylons she was wearing. Behind her, Abel leaped gracefully into the back seat.

"Mom looked happy tonight," Riley said as he started the engine. It purred to life, rumbling beneath them. He pulled out of his mother's driveway, the tires crunching over the snowy gravel.

Mila smiled and reached over to squeeze his hand on the gearshift. "She seemed to like her present. I'm glad we went with that carved crystal ball stand."

From the back seat, came Abel's scathing two cents. "I don't know how such a venerable witch can have such low standards with her familiar."

Riley, also an old-time enemy of Myron, scoffed, "You and me both, pal."

After that little jab and Riley's endorsement, the black cat began to groom himself, his pink tongue lapping at his inky fur. Mila glanced at him in the rearview mirror. Despite his prim demeanor, she knew he secretly loved his verbal sparring with Glenda's familiar.

Riley merged onto the main road, the speedometer needle climbing higher... and higher. Mila raised an eyebrow.

"In a bit of a rush, are we?" she asked, her voice echoing teasingly through their mental bond. "Shouldn't magical law enforcement officers lead by example and respect the speed limits?"

Riley's lips quirked in a half-smile, but he kept his eyes on the road ahead. *"What can I say? I'm eager to get my wife home."*

Mila chuckled softly as the car sped through the quiet streets. She glanced over at Riley, admiring the way his strong hands gripped the steering wheel, the determined set of his jaw. She reached out through their bond again. *"You mean you're eager to see this in person?"* She sent him a quick reminder of the tantalizing image that she'd shown him at dinner of herself draped in red lace lingerie, the delicate fabric barely concealing her curves.

Riley inhaled sharply, his knuckles turning white. "You're killing me, my love," he growled through their mental link. "I haven't been able to think about anything else all through dinner."

Mila grinned, reveling in the love that flowed so freely between them. And that, in over a year together, hadn't dimmed one bit. Only intensified. *"Good. That was the plan."*

From the backseat came an abrupt hissing noise. Mila turned to see Abel glaring at them, his yellow eyes narrowed. "Are you two talking through your bond again?" he asked prissily.

Riley cleared his throat. "Uh, yes. Sorry, Abel."

The cat sniffed. "Just talking? Or are you engaging in mental foreplay, intending to copulate the moment we arrive home?"

Mila burst out laughing at the scandalized expression on Abel's face. "Don't worry, I have to put away the turkey leftovers before any copulating can occur."

"Screw the leftovers," Riley muttered under his breath, sending Mila a smoldering look that set her blood on fire.

She bit her lip, struggling to maintain her composure. If Abel weren't in the car with them, she might've moved her teasing out of the strictly mental playfield they were restrained to now. She imagined dragging her hand over his muscular thigh unhurriedly and—

"Stop that, or we're going to crash," Riley shot a raw plea through their bond.

Mila smiled. "I thought a Chief

Inquisitor should be more disciplined to work under pressure."

Riley's response didn't come in words this time. He deployed his aerial hands, sinking them into her hair, massaging her scalp, trailing them down her neck, over her collarbones, and down her upper arms. Then he became naughtier.

Mila had to bite her lower lip not to whimper. But apparently, her stealth skills weren't up to par.

"At least wait until we're at home," came Abel's alarmed protest. Her familiar sighed heavily.

Mila turned to her husband, who was still fondling her, and mentally surrendered. *"You've made your point, Inquisitor."*

Riley smirked. Clearly satisfied. He didn't drop his aerial hands entirely though; he moved them over Mila's shoulders, massaging the knots in her back in a way that—if more chaste—was still delicious. She might've started to purr. Quite the opposite state of mind of her cat.

Abel let out a deep, throaty noise that expressed displeasure. "It is far too cold a night to be ousted from the warmth of one's home simply so one's witch can indulge her carnal desires with her soulmate."

Mila rolled her eyes, turning to face her familiar. "That's why you have a magically heated shed in the backyard, Abel. It's perfectly cozy in there."

The cat's ears flattened against his head. "Be that as it may, I do not appreciate being unceremoniously evicted from my rightful place by the hearth."

A sly smile curved Mila's lips. "Besides, it's not as if you're always alone in that shed. I seem to recall spotting a certain bushy-tailed Siberian beauty slinking out of there on more than one occasion."

Abel's eyes widened, and he began to vigorously lick his paw, his sleek fur bristling with indignation. "I sure don't know what you're implying." He sniffed. "A true gentlecat doesn't kiss and tell."

Riley chuckled, glancing at Mila with a knowing grin. "You mean your stuck-up familiar has been having a secret tryst with the neighbor's cat?" he teased through their bond.

"Apparently so," Mila replied, amusement sparkling in her thoughts. "And here I thought he spent his evenings contemplating the mysteries of the universe."

"Well, he is a cat, after all. They're inscrutable creatures."

As the car turned onto their street, the journey nearing its end, Mila leaned back, letting herself enjoy the last few moments of the drive. They pulled into the driveway and the enchantments woven into their home greeted them with a soft, welcoming glow. Riley, having seen more dark magic than most wizards, was a bit of a security freak. When he'd moved in, he'd been appalled Mila had no wards of any kind at her house and promptly spun about a thousand around the tiny house.

The moment Riley killed the engine, Abel leaped from the backseat with a dignified huff, his black fur rippling beneath the moonlight as he made a beeline for his heated shed, tail held high. Mila and Riley watched him go, their bond humming with amusement at the feline display of disapproval.

They started up the driveway. Riley carrying the mountain of food Glenda had saddled them with, and Mila already searching in her purse for the keys.

As they got into the house, Mila flipped on the lights with a flick of her finger. Riley pointedly dimmed them with his own magic to near-total obscurity, the soft glow barely illuminating their faces. He unceremoniously dropped the leftovers he was carrying on the floor with a thud and pulled his wife into his powerful arms.

"Happy anniversary," he murmured, nuzzling her neck, his breath warm against her skin. "I can't believe it's only a year since we met."

Mila chuckled, tilting her head to give him better access even as amusement colored her tone. "You mean you can't believe it's only a year since you burst into my house, stunned me, and then brutally and unjustifiably arrested me?" The memories of her life before Riley—the loneliness, the hopelessness that had brought her to brew a love potion—were now only a distant haze.

Riley pulled back, brow furrowed in exasperation. "*I* didn't stun you."

"Puh-TAY-toh, puh-TAH-toh," Mila replied breezily, waving a hand—she loved riling him up about the night they first met. "I still ended up in a pink robe and shackles." She stared at the mug shot Riley had framed and lovingly placed over the mantel. Not her finest moment.

But Riley just grinned, unrepentant, and went back to kissing down the column of her throat. "The most beautiful criminal I ever saw," he said, voice muffled against her skin.

"I have to say, you playing bad cop has grown on me."

He arched a mischievous eyebrow. "Oh, yeah? Let's see what I can do."

Her husband grazed his teeth over her neck and bit down harder than usual.

Mila shivered at the touch of his lips, the timbre of his words. Who would have thought that disastrous first meeting would lead them here—husband and wife, captor and captive turned equals and lovers. It still amazed her sometimes, even as she melted against him, the rest of the world fading away. In his arms, she was home.

Mila pressed into Riley's embrace, catching his lips with her own in a passionate kiss. His mouth was hot and insistent against hers as his hands roamed over her back and her sides, igniting sparks across her skin even through the fabric of her dress. She tangled her fingers in his hair, holding him close, savoring the solid strength of him, the heady taste of him.

Magic swirled around them, adding an extra layer of sensation—a tingle here, a caress there, stoked by the rising heat between them. Mila felt her own power reaching out to twine with Riley's, silver and gold, fire and ice, yin and yang. Perfect complements, in magic, as in life.

They parted just long enough to eliminate the pesky barrier of clothing. Mila's dress vanished with a flick of Riley's wrist. His shirt disappeared next, courtesy of her undressing spell—one she had a lot of practice with over the last year.

Mila ran appreciative hands over the sculpted planes of her husband's chest, reveling in the freedom to touch, the knowledge that this was hers, that *he* was hers, now and always. No more secrets, no more walls—just skin against skin, heart against heart.

Riley's hands were equally busy mapping her curves. Mila arched into the touch, head falling back on a gasp, the sensations magnified by the curl of his magic around her.

"I love you," he murmured against her throat, the words a brand, a vow. "My beautiful, brilliant, infuriating witch."

"I love you too," she breathed, the truth of it pulsing through her veins, bright and fierce and eternal. "My stubborn, arrogant, wonderful Inquisitor."

He laughed, low and wicked, and swept her up into his arms, carrying her toward the bedroom. Mila wrapped herself around him, dizzy with need and love and sheer, incandescent happiness.

It didn't matter how they'd begun. All that mattered was this, now, the two of them, the life they'd built from the ashes of that first tumultuous meeting. She'd go through it all again, a thousand times over, if it meant having this. Having him.

Always.

He laid her down gently on the plush comforter. With a tender kiss on her forehead, he crawled in beside her, pulling her close. They made love, fast and furious the first time, then more tenderly. Until Mila could only manage a breathless laugh, her entire body alight with sensation as their heartbeats gradually slowed to normal.

Exhausted and lightheaded from the force of their passion, she snuggled against her husband's chest, listening to the steady drum of his heartbeat as it lulled her toward slumber. Tangled together, content and at peace in each other's embrace, they drifted off to sleep—two halves of one whole, bound by a love that transcended any magic.

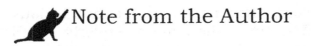Note from the Author

Dear Reader,

I hope you enjoyed reading Don't Kiss and Spell. If you enjoyed spending time in this magical world, I'm happy to let you know this story has a sequel, **A Match Made in Coven.**

The second book in the series follows Agent Sarah Michelle Callidora as she tackles a gruesome murder case alongside self-proclaimed amateur detective Lorcan Black. Working with a civilian is challenging enough, but to add insult to injury, Lorcan belongs to a rival coven, nursing a centuries-old grudge against the Callidora clan. Spending time with him proves almost unbearable— particularly because of his infuriating charm and good looks.

Turn the page to read an excerpt from this new chapter in the series.

Now, I have to ask you a favor. If you loved my story, **please leave a review** on your favorite retailer website, Goodreads, Bookbub, or wherever you like to post reviews (your blog, your Facebook wall, your bedroom wall, in a text to your best friend... a BookTok or Bookstagram video!). Reviews are the best gift you can give to an author, and word of mouth is the most powerful means of book discovery.

Thank you for your constant support!

Camilla, x

Chapter 1

Killer Overtime

SARAH MICHELLE

Agent Callidora's breath fogged the chilly fall night air as she ducked under the yellow police tape. A week before Halloween, the streets of Salem buzzed with anticipation—the townsfolk unaware of the gruesome scene hidden away in a downtown office building.

A fellow magical enforcer greeted her on the other side of the tape with a curt, "Detective." He added a grim nod. "This one's something to see."

Sarah Michelle grunted in acknowledgment; her mind was still groggy from being jolted awake by the call less than half an hour before. It wasn't the first time her job had abruptly interrupted her sleep, and it wouldn't be the last.

Stepping inside the victim's office, the metallic scent of blood assaulted her senses, chasing away any lingering fogs of drowsiness. Several officers from Salem Magical Police Department (SMPD) were on site, their expressions bleak and professional as they filed away evidences. The crime scene photographer moved around methodically, capturing every angle of the room, while a forensic specialist examined the area with a wand emitting a soft blue light, looking for potential spell residues.

And in the center of it all, slumped over his desk, was the victim, Elijah Preston, a magical blade plunged deep into the back of his skull, the eerie glow of the weapon casting sinister shadows on his lifeless face.

"Blasted trolls," Sarah Michelle muttered under her breath as she approached the body, her eyes narrowing. The dagger was unlike any she had encountered before, crafted from golden metal engraved with intricate magical swirls. It pulsed with a persistent throb of power that seemed to synchronize with each beat of her heart.

She leaned closer, studying the symbols etched into the bejeweled handle. They were ancient, complex. She was looking at an old, expensive artifact that only a few families in Salem could afford to purchase. Or an heirloom—even better, easier to track.

"Looks like our man stumbled into

something too big for him," Sarah Michelle remarked dryly to no one in particular. The victim might be human, but this was no ordinary murder.

As she straightened up, her gaze fell on a photograph on Preston's desk. It showed him shaking hands with a strikingly handsome man, their smiles wide. Sarah Michelle's breath caught in her throat as something about the tall, blond guy in the picture drew her in. She had to resist the instinct to pick up the photo and have a closer look—not until forensics was done. But she kept studying the man's chiseled features and piercing blue-green eyes. Even through the glossy paper, she could sense an undeniable aura of power surrounding him. Her gut told her this mysterious stranger was a wizard.

As the coroner came in to move the body, she exited the office to take a breath of air that didn't smell like death. The space was already too crowded.

In contrast, the headquarters of Cornerstone Constructions, likely a bustling hub of activity during the day, were now ominously silent. Desks were neatly arranged, but papers lay scattered as if someone had searched them and then abandoned the quest in haste.

Beyond the glass, the world carried on as if nothing had happened, the muted din of the street outside providing a mundane backdrop to the macabre scene.

Sarah approached the attending officer, a seasoned veteran named Flint, and set down to do the legwork of the investigation. "What do we know so far?"

Officer Flint glanced up from his notepad. "Not much yet, Detective. Preston was found by the cleaning crew when they came in as they do every night at eleven P.M. No signs of forced entry."

"No magical or human infractions?" Sarah Michelle pressed.

"No, the place had no enchanted wards to infract upon, and it looks like the victim let the killer in."

"Ah, so they knew each other."

"Most probably."

"Any idea what kind of magic we're dealing with?" She asked, gesturing toward the shimmering knife that was being retrieved before the body could be moved.

Flint shook his head. "Never seen anything like it. We'll have to take it to the lab for analysis."

Sarah Michelle's eyes narrowed on the agent carrying the still-glowing blade away in a plastic bag. The flashing lights of the police cruisers outside the glass building illuminated his path, casting a red and blue glow across the pavement. She turned to Officer Flint, her voice crisp. "Time of death?"

He consulted his notes. "Medical examiner estimates at ten P.M."

"Any suspects seen entering or leaving the building around that hour?" Sarah asked, her gaze scanning the perimeter.

"None so far. But the cameras were disabled, by someone with a code."

"The victim?"

"Possible. Or someone else with access."

Sarah Michelle's brow furrowed. *Interesting.* "Did Elijah Preston have any known involvement with the magical community?"

Flint hesitated, shifting his weight. "Well, turns out his business partner is a wizard."

Her pulse quickened—thoughts immediately jumping to the handsome man in the photo. She fixed her colleague with a penetrating stare. "Do we have a name?"

"Yes, ma'am. He's..." Flint hesitated, then he replied with a resigned sigh. "Lorcan Black."

The name hit Sarah like a stunner to the chest. The good-looking wizard was a Black. Countless warnings rang in her ears—hushed whispers around the dinner table at family gatherings of betrayal, subterfuge, cruelty... and *murder*. The Blacks and the Callidoras had been enemy covens for centuries, ever since an alliance through marriage had ended in a blood bath instead.

Sarah Michelle's mind whirled as she processed the information. The idea of working on an investigation involving a Black made her skin crawl, but she had to remain professional. She inhaled calmly, pushing down the surge of emotions. This was not the time to get caught up in ancient feuds. She had a case to solve. Schooling her features into a neutral expression, she refocused on Flint. "I need everything you have on Black. His whereabouts, his alibi, any connection he might have to the murder weapon."

Flint nodded, his demeanor guarded. "I'll get right on it. But Sarah Michelle..." He hesitated as if weighing his words. "Be careful with this one. The Blacks are a powerful coven, and they don't take kindly to being crossed."

Sarah Michelle's lips curved into a humorless smile. "Neither do the Callidoras." She spun around, already studying her next move. She needed to talk to Lorcan Black, to look him in the eye and gauge his reaction to the news of Preston's death. But first, better to do her homework.

She pulled out her phone and dialed a familiar number. "Hey, it's me," she said when the call connected. "I need a favor. Can you pull up everything we have on Lorcan Black? ... Yeah, I know it's late. But this is important." She listened for a moment, then nodded. "Not even a citation? A minor misdemeanor?" The colleague she trusted the most for profiling suspects confirmed that Black was squeaky clean—or his family had wiped out every trace of wrongdoing. "Thanks," she said into the phone. "I owe you one."

As she hung up the call, Sarah was already piecing together theories and possible motives—a woman they both wanted, an argument about money, the usual. Was Lorcan Black a violent type? If his public profile was immaculate, she'd have to dig deeper to find some dirt on him, if it existed.

A Callidora and a Black, linked by a

murder. Oh, this case was going to be a doozy, no doubt about it. But Sarah Michelle was never one to back down from a challenge. Even if it came in the form of an attractive potentially murderous wizard from a rival coven.

She was still mulling over the new development when another officer approached, holding a clipboard with details about the murder weapon. The junior agent, his uniform slightly askew, handed the clipboard to Flint with a deferential nod.

Flint scanned the report, his eyebrows climbing higher with each line. He looked up at Sarah, an unreadable expression on his face. "The magical dagger lodged in Preston's skull? It's registered to Lorcan Black."

Ah. Lorcan's blade had been found in the victim's head—his business partner. No infractions, so the killer was let in, *or had a key*. While the cameras had been disabled by someone with the codes. It was almost too neat, too obvious. But Sarah knew better than to dismiss the evidences staring her in the face.

Nailing a Black for murder would bring double satisfaction. Justice would be served and her family vindicated.

Lorcan Black. The name tasted bitter on her tongue, like a poorly brewed potion. She'd spent her entire life hearing about the Blacks, about their viciousness. But not just that, their entitlement, and the injustices they had inflicted. And now, fate had thrown her right into the middle of it.

But Sarah prided herself on upholding her integrity. She wouldn't condemn the wizard based solely on his family name. She couldn't let personal history cloud her judgment, not when there was a killer to catch. With a final, resolute look at Officer Flint, she turned on her heel, her voice calm but icy.

"Prepare a warrant. We're going to pay Mr. Black a visit."

ooo

Dive into a world of magic, mystery, and unexpected romance! Join Lorcan and Sarah Michelle as they unravel secrets, trade barbs, and follow a trail of clues that brings them closer to danger—and each other.

About the Author

Camilla is an engineer who left science behind to enter the whimsical realm of romantic fiction.

She writes contemporary rom-coms. Her characters have big hearts, might be a little stubborn at times, and love to banter with each other. Every story she pens has a guaranteed HEA that will make your heart beat faster. Unless you're a vampire, of course.

She's a cat lover, coffee addict, and shoe hoarder. Besides writing, she loves reading—duh!—cooking, watching bad TV, and going to the movies—popcorn, please! She's a bit of a foodie, nothing too serious. A keen traveler, Camilla knows mosquitoes play a role in the ecosystem, and she doesn't want to starve all those frog princes out there, but she could really live without them.

camillaisley.com

Made in the USA
Las Vegas, NV
12 October 2024

96721823R00167